...**eans a lot to**

They mean a lot to me, she wanted to say. *I miss them. I miss you. I miss what we had, what we started to have.*

"Rehearsals start tomorrow," she told him, forcing herself to be all business. "Three thirty to five thirty. Monday, Wednesday and Friday will be the regular schedule. I'm putting out the call for volunteers tomorrow, so the twins and other little ones will be in good hands."

He nodded. "I'm sure they will be. I'll make sure they're there." He was looking everywhere but at her. "Boys," he called, "let's get home for that ice cream I promised you."

As they walked out, each holding one of Logan's hands, that empty feeling came crawling back. What she would give to be with Logan and the boys in his living room, laughing over something silly and eating ice cream.

How was she going to handle seeing Logan Grainger six times a week for five seconds at a time?

* * *

Hurley's Homestyle Kitchen:

THE COWBOY'S
BIG FAMILY TREE

BY
MEG MAXWELL

First Published in Great Britain 2016
By Mills & Boon, an imprint of HarperCollins*Publishers*
1 London Bridge Street, London, SE1 9GF

© 2016 Meg Maxwell

ISBN: 978-0-263-92036-9

23-1116

Our policy is to use papers that are natural, renewable and recyclable products and made from wood grown in sustainable forests. The logging and manufacturing processes conform to the legal environmental regulations of the country of origin.

Printed and bound in Spain
by CPI, Barcelona

Meg Maxwell lives on the coast of Maine with her teenage son, their beagle and their black-and-white cat. When she's not writing, Meg is either reading, at the movies or thinking up new story ideas on her favorite little beach (even in winter) just minutes from her house. Interesting fact: Meg Maxwell is a pseudonym for author Melissa Senate, whose women's fiction titles have been published in over twenty-five countries.

For my beloved Max

Chapter One

I don't know if you were ever informed or not, Logan, but your biological father was not Haywood Grainger. I know this because I am your biological father. I cannot bear to leave this world without making sure you know the truth...

As much as Logan Grainger had tried to put the stranger's letter out of his mind since receiving it three months ago, the deathbed confession crept into his head all the time. During early morning chores in the barn as he cleaned horse stalls and laid out fresh hay. When he woke up his three-year-old nephews for breakfast, their uncle Logan all they had in the world. As he rode acres of fence, wondering how much longer he could ignore the truth. The supposed truth. After all, Logan hadn't tried to verify the man's claims.

Because he couldn't deal with it. And because everything pointed to it being true. Logan was six foot two. His father was five foot eight, his mother a petite four eleven. His parents were both blond. Logan's hair was dark. At least he knew where his blue eye color came from: his mother, even if neither of his parents shared his Clint Eastwood squint.

When people used to marvel at how Logan looked so little like his parents or his younger brother, his mother would quickly say, *Oh, he's a Grainger through and through*.

Except according to a letter from one Clyde T. Parsons, Logan was the result of a brief romance between him and Logan's mother, before his mother married his dad. Clyde had gotten her in the family way, then freaked out and walked out on her, leaving her alone and pregnant in a small town. Had Haywood Grainger known his mother was pregnant when he married her? Had he known their firstborn son wasn't his?

If he had, his father hadn't shown it.

I am your father. I am your father. I am your father.

Those damned words from Parsons's letter circled around his head all the time. He'd feel it hard in his gut about himself—*who am I? Who the heck is Clyde Parsons?* And then he'd look at his boys, the sweet, innocent orphaned nephews he was raising, and he'd feel it harder about them and what it meant.

Was he even their uncle? If Parsons was telling the truth and Logan wasn't a Grainger, were Harry and Henry even really his? *No matter what, you're still your mother's son*, he reminded himself for the millionth time since getting that letter. *So if Parsons is your biological father, you're your brother's half sibling. Which makes you the twins' half uncle.*

Screw that, he thought. There was nothing half about his relationship with his nephews.

"Watch, Uncle Logan!" Henry, the older twin by one minute, twelve seconds, called out, knocking Logan from his thoughts. The little boy raced across the barn and flung himself into a pile of hay.

Next to the small evergreen set up in a corner near the door, Harry was twirling himself in red tinsel meant for the tree, then followed his brother in a running leap for the haystack.

Logan closed his eyes for a moment—never a good idea with three-year-olds running amok—and put down the box of ornaments he'd found in the attic. *They're yours,* he assured himself again, opening his eyes to see the boys pulling hay out of their thick blond hair. A whole bunch of legal paperwork said so. When Logan's brother, Seth, and his wife, Mandy, died in a private plane crash last spring, Logan had been named legal guardian of his nephews. Mandy had no family and all Seth had was a wild older brother who lived and breathed for the rodeo circuit.

But when Logan had gotten the news about Seth's death nine months ago, he'd quit the rodeo, quit the road, quit it all, and had come home to Blue Gulch. He'd picked up where Seth had left off, on the ranch his brother had fought so hard to hang on to. Logan had put a good chunk of his considerable savings into the place over the last nine months and he was proud of the strong, healthy herd, the new barn and the new roof on the farm-house. The Grainger Ranch was the boys' legacy and Logan would not only keep it going, but build it into something grand for them. In the meantime, though, he'd ensure the twins a good Christmas—their first without their parents. Today was the last day of November, the day he'd promised Harry and Henry they could finally decorate the barn tree for the horses.

"Uncle Logan, can I put a snowflake on Lulu's door?" Harry asked, pulling a tattered, folded origami snow-flake that he'd made in preschool that morning from his pocket. He pointed at the mare's stall.

"Sure can," Logan said.

Henry raced over, his little body covered in hay. He pulled out his own tattered snowflake and Logan helped them tape them up on the low wall of the stall.

"Do the horses know Christmas is coming?" Harry asked, his big pale brown eyes so like his father's.

Logan scooped up one boy in each arm, balancing each against a hip. "Do you think so?"

"Yes," Harry said.

"Me too," Henry added, those same big brown eyes full of surety.

Logan smiled. "I think so too. Let's go into the house and have that ice cream I promised you," he added, giv-ing each a kiss and setting them down. "We'll finish decorating the barn tree tomorrow."

"Can Clementine come help?" Henry asked.

"I miss her," Harry said.

Clementine Hurley's pretty face flashed into his mind, her long, silky dark hair always caught in a ponytail, her big hazel eyes with all those lashes, the way she filled out a white T-shirt and jeans.

He let her image linger for a second, then forced it away.

"No, guys," he said gently, knowing how much they liked their former babysitter.

He'd never forget the last time she sat for the boys, back in August. He'd come into the house, done for the day, looking forward to seeing the twins and her, but the boys had fallen asleep on the couch as she'd read them a story so she'd been waiting for him to come in to bring them up to bed. He did, tucking them in, regretful that he hadn't been able to say good-night. When he came back down, all Clementine had done was ask him how things had gone with the calf he'd been keeping an eye on, and all of a sudden he kissed her. Just tilted up her chin with his hand and leaned forward and kissed her. She'd kissed him back too. Hard.

He'd stepped back, unsure if he wanted to start something with Clementine after the debacle he'd been through on the rodeo circuit with Bethany, aka The Liar. Bethany Appleton had cost him his trust in himself, his reputation and his livelihood, though for a month he'd been a hot ticket, folks coming out in droves to see the Handcuff Cowboy in the ring. That bullcrud aside, the night he'd kissed Clementine, he'd only had the twins for a few months and wanted to focus on them and getting the ranch in order, not on romance.

She'd seemed to sense his unease and had said, "Oh, I ran into the mailman outside and he gave me your mail." She'd scooped up the pile from the coffee table.

He wanted to stall so he'd glanced at the stack of mail, all bills he'd take care of. But one was from a name he didn't recognize, a Tuckerville, Texas, return address.

"I should open this," he'd said, needing a minute to think about the kiss. Did he really want to start down this road again? Pre-Bethany, he'd been open to love and marriage and all that warm and fuzzy stuff he observed from a distance at holidays and birthday celebrations with his brother's family. Post-Bethany, he was cynical and wary about what ugliness might be hidden inside pretty packages. With Clementine eyeing him, he'd pretended great interest in opening the letter, fully expecting it to be nothing, junk mail even.

But it was from Clyde T. Parsons with a damned bombshell.

The color must have drained from his face and his expression must have been grim because Clementine had rushed over to him and asked if everything was okay.

"No," he'd said. "It's not. I need you to go."

He was surprised, to this day, that her expression had registered. Hurt. Confusion. But it had. He'd just been too shocked to try to fix it, soften it. She'd nodded, then went to the door and looked back at him, his gaze on the letter, reading it again and a third time. He felt her eyes on him, but he hadn't looked up; he'd just turned away and she'd left, the door clicking shut behind her.

And then all thought of Clementine Hurley, of anything, went out of his mind.

His entire life had been a lie. He wasn't a Grainger. He wasn't his father's son. People he'd loved had lied to him.

And a stranger, a man claiming to be his biological father, had told him the damned truth.

If it *was* the truth, Logan thought now, holding out a hand to each nephew. But why would the man lie? Deathbed confessions didn't work that way. People told the truth to settle stuff inside them, to make things right, to go in peace, to get into heaven.

As each little nephew slipped a tiny, trusting hand into his, Logan felt that same burn in his gut. *Who the hell am I?*

And was he going to ignore the letter as he'd done the past three months? Not follow up? Not confirm whether it was true? He thought about the little gold key that had been in the envelope and the next to last paragraph of Parsons's letter.

> *I've never had much money, but every week since you were born until you turned eighteen I put money away for you, child support, I suppose, in a PO box at the post office in Tuckerville where I live. Eighteen years times fifty two weeks adds up, but I have no idea how much is in there. Some weeks I had five bucks to put in, some weeks fifty if there was overtime. But I never skipped a week, not once. I want you to know that.*

Logan didn't want to know that. He didn't want to know any of it.

The next day, he'd told Clementine he wouldn't be needing her to sit for him anymore. And then he'd shut her out. He'd shut out everyone, not that there were so many people in his life these days. His parents had been gone almost ten years and Logan had always been one to keep to himself.

There had been a warm outpouring of support for him in those early months after he'd come home to raise the boys. Clementine, who he'd known only as the startlingly pretty waitress at Hurley's Homestyle Kitchen, where he'd liked to have lunch as often as possible, had come by the house to pay her respects with a heap of food in containers with reheating instructions and enough homemade pies to last him a year. He'd ignored his attraction to Clementine and took her up on her offer to babysit whenever he needed. And there she'd been, in his house, and they'd gotten to know each other some, Logan leaving out all that had happened that final month on the rodeo circuit. Clementine Hurley had been through quite a bit herself, and he'd been so drawn to her that keeping himself from kissing her had taken restraint he didn't know he had. Until he'd been unable to stop himself and kissed her.

That was finished now. Logan's universe was his nephews, the land, the livestock and anyone connected to the twins, like their preschool teacher and pediatrician, the nice children's librarian at the public library and Miss Karen, the grandmotherly sitter he'd hired to replace Clementine. Some small talk with those people, and Logan could go back to necessary isolation, to finding a space he could exist between trying to make sense of the letter and forgetting it entirely. After Bethany, then losing his brother and then the letter, Logan was done, just plain done. He wanted as much distance between himself and the rest of the world as possible.

And the rest of the world at this point was really just one person: Clementine Hurley. She made him want things he was trying so hard not to want, not to think about or care about. He thought people couldn't be trusted *before* he'd gotten Parsons's letter? Logan had had no idea that the truth of your existence, how you came about in the world, who shared your blood, your DNA, could be just wiped clean. That your own parents, your good, kind, hardworking parents, could withhold something so vital, so fundamental.

That you weren't who you always thought you were. Sometimes late at night, when Logan would try to wrap his mind around what burned him most, that seemed to be it.

"I wish Clementine could come help us decorate the tree," Henry said. "I like Miss Karen, but I like Clementine better."

"Me too," Harry said.

Logan sighed inwardly, hating that he was depriving the boys of someone who meant so much to them. And with so much loss in their young lives, he'd taken her away from them and it wasn't fair. The twins hadn't seen Clementine since a few days after he'd fired her when Henry had gotten lost in the woods for a very scary half hour and Clementine had been part of the search party. They'd lit up at the sight of her and asked about her often.

Wait a minute. He stopped in his tracks and pulled a folded-up flyer from his back pocket. He'd almost forgotten.

*Children of Blue Gulch, ages 2–17! Come try
out for the Children's Christmas Spectacular.
Blue Gulch Town Hall. 3:30–5:30. Auditions held
Wednesday and Thursday. Director: Clementine
Hurley...*

He glanced at his watch. It was Thursday and 5:25.
If he hurried, he might just make it. His boys could be
in the show and have their time with Clementine *off*
Logan's turf.

"Hey, guys," Logan said on the way out of the barn.
"Remember when I asked last week if you two want to be
in the town Christmas show? Would you like to audition
tonight? You have to sing 'Jingle Bells.'"

He'd taught them the song the past week, ever since
the flyers had gone up. But they couldn't remember anything past "Jingle Bells" and sometimes the words *way*
and *sleigh.* Heck, they were only three.

"Jingle bells, jingle—" Henry started, then scrunched
up his face.

"Uncle Logan, what comes after jingle the second
time?" Harry asked.

Logan smiled. Clementine had her work cut out for
her. But he wouldn't have to deal with her in his house,
in his living room, in his kitchen or fantasize about her
being in his bedroom. Three times a week for a few
weeks, he'd drop off the twins at the Blue Gulch town
hall, pick them up and that would be that. The kiss was
a thing of the past.

When you didn't know who the hell you were, when

your trust in the people who'd been closest to you had been obliterated, how could you open up your life to someone? You couldn't.

Clementine Hurley listened to the little girl sing the first stanza of "Jingle Bells," her heart about to burst. Emma was just five years old and she'd stumbled over the words *bob tails ring* as almost every kid Clementine "auditioned" had.

Emma hung her head, her eyes filling with tears and she stopped singing.

Clementine rushed up to the stage in the community room of the town hall. "Hey," she soothed. "You were doing great! Bob tails ring doesn't exactly flow off the tongue."

"But I don't get to be in the show, right?" Emma said, her blue eyes teary. "I messed up."

"You do get to be in the show," Clementine assured her. "Every kid who tries out for the Blue Gulch Children's Christmas Spectacular gets a part. Every single one," she added, touching a finger to Emma's nose.

Emma's face brightened. "Can I try the song again?"

"Sure can," Clementine said, smiling. She headed back to her seat, a folding chair a few feet from the stage.

She glanced at the short line of kids still waiting to audition. Between yesterday and today, Clementine had listened to over thirty kids sing the first two stanzas of "Jingle Bells." Five kids left and then she could start organizing the holiday show into parts. The woman who usually directed the kids' show had become a full-time caregiver for her ailing mother and had no time for extras. She'd asked Clementine, known around town for being an ace babysitter and great with kids of all ages, to step in and she had, without hesitation. Clementine had accepted for a few reasons. Now twenty-five years old, Clementine herself had been in the town's children's Christmas show since she was old enough to remember, so not only was she familiar with how the show worked, it was a nice way for her to give back to the community. And anything that would keep her mind off Logan Grainger was a good thing. The holiday show would keep her very, very busy.

Too busy to think of a very handsome rancher with thick dark hair, blue eyes that made her forget what day it was and a kindness with the young nephews he was raising that had once made her cry. She'd fallen hard for Logan Grainger, so hard and so deeply, and when he'd finally, finally, finally kissed her, she'd almost melted in a puddle on the floor. She'd felt a joy inside her in that moment that she'd never before felt. And then fifteen seconds later, it was all over. *All* over. The kiss. The hope. The maybe. Her job as his sitter.

All she knew was that he'd gotten a letter that had changed something. He'd gone from the usual Logan, albeit one who finally kissed her after a few months of very clear chemistry between them, to closed off. She'd tried many times to talk to him, to get him to talk to her, to tell her what was going on, to let her back in. But he wouldn't. That was three months ago.

"With a bellbell bell and a—" Emma sang, the tears starting again.

Aww. The first two stanzas of "Jingle Bells" were a

lot to remember for little kids. "I have an idea," Clementine said, standing up and going back over to the stage. "Let's sing it together, then you'll try it one more time."

Clementine knelt down and took Emma's hand. "And a one and a two and a… Dashing through the snow, in a one-horse open sleigh, o'er the fields we go, laughing all the way, bells on bob tails ring, making spirits bright, what fun it is to ride and sing, a sleighing song tonight. Oh, jingle bells, jingle bells, jingle all the way, oh what fun it is to ride in a one-horse open sleigh."

Clementine held up her hand, palm out. "High five, kiddo. You did it! Now you try again, just you."

Emma sang the bob tails ring part just right that time, then ran over to Clementine's assistant for the show, Louisa Perkins, who also happened to be the foster mother at the group home where Emma lived. All six foster children had auditioned. Just as Clementine had when she was a foster kid in Blue Gulch before Charlaine and Clinton Hurley had taken her in and then adopted her. Clementine admired Louisa, amazed the woman gave so much of her time. Clementine had been in a few foster homes, one decent, two not so good, and it warmed her heart to know Louisa and her husband were wonderful parents to kids who needed them.

Clementine sat back down in her chair and called up the next child to audition.

"…bells on bob tails ring…" the ten-year-old sang without a hitch.

Clementine breathed a sigh of relief. The holiday show would have ten songs and a short play, an original about the founding of Blue Gulch on Christmas Eve back in 1885. The town's residents loved the annual show, even if everyone had seen it a thousand times over the past twenty-five years, ever since a beloved drama teacher from the high school had written the play and started the town tradition. Clementine had a few big parts to fill for some of the speaking roles and she'd just found her Lila-Mae.

"Bells on bobcats ring," the next boy sang, and Clementine had to smile. It had been long day and it was going to be a long night, but she adored kids and come the show on Christmas Eve, these kids would be singing bob tails ring just right. Or not, she knew. Perfect lyrics didn't matter to Clementine. It was all about trying, about effort, about showing up and wanting to be part of something special. That was what Clementine wanted to teach these kids.

As the boy continued to bungle the song, Clementine's heart went out to him.

"Jingle bells, Batman smells, Robin laid an egg," the boy sang, then burst into anxious giggles.

"Sillybones," Clementine said, tsking a finger at him. But she laughed too. "From the top, young man."

He smiled and nodded and sang it again, even getting bob tails ring right.

Three more auditions later, and Clementine was finished. She had the dinner shift at Hurley's Homestyle Kitchen ahead of her, then needed to work on the Creole sauce that she was perfecting and afterward she could look forward to an hour-long soak in a hot bath. It was Thursday, and every day this week she'd spent an hour at the foster home working with the kids to learn the song, then had done her waitressing shifts at Hurley's, then babysat all over town for infants and toddlers and small and big kids. Clementine had a twofold reason for all the babysitting. She was on her way to fulfilling a dream she'd had since she was a teenager, since the Hurley family had taken her in from that not-so-great foster care situation. Clementine was working toward becoming a foster mother herself. She'd gone to the many meetings, done the thirty-five hours and then some of training, gotten additional training in medicines and CPR and first aid, and completed the home study with her supportive grandmother at her side.

Soon, a child—whether an infant, a toddler, a little kid, a tween or teen—would come to live with Clementine in the home she shared with her grandmother, the apricot Victorian on Blue Gulch Street that also housed their fifty-year-old restaurant, Hurley's Homestyle Kitchen. She'd shower that child with the love and care she'd been provided when her parents had taken her in. She was hoping that her final paperwork would be signed off very soon so that she could be matched with a girl or boy before Christmas. Oh, did she want to give her foster child a very special Christmas.

The other reason Clementine babysat so much was because she was trying to earn extra money to surprise her grandmother with a Christmas present—an outdoor dining section in her beloved garden. And she had just enough to ask her friend, a female contractor, to start work on the project right after the busy holidays. Hurley's was doing a lot better than it had been just six months ago, especially thanks to her sister Annabel's generous husband, West. But Essie Hurley, who'd opened the restaurant in her home as a newlywed fifty years ago, refused to take any more of West's money now that Hurley's was making a small profit. All Essie wanted was to stay open, pay her bills, make payroll and have some left over for an emergency fund. Clementine couldn't wait till she could tell Essie about her present. When Clementine's parents had died in a car crash when Clementine was thirteen, Essie had taken in her three orphaned granddaughters, and as always, she'd made Clementine feel like an equal part of the family as she had from the moment she'd met Clementine at age eight. Clementine wanted to do something special for her gram.

Finally, the community room was empty and Clementine packed up her folder of lyric sheets and slid it in her tote bag. She glanced around the room, suddenly feeling very much alone. Last summer, when Logan had broken her heart by shutting her out, her sisters, both older and wiser than Clementine, had advised her to fill her life with what she loved doing. So she had, volunteering at the foster home, working toward the foster parent requirements, babysitting, helping her family in the kitchen between her shifts and now directing the town's children's play. But still, when she was alone, like right now, she still felt a strange emptiness, something inside her was still raw. Heartbreak? Longing?

"Uh-oh, boys, I think we're too late."

There was no mistaking the voice that came from outside the door to the community room. Logan Grainger. He'd been avoiding her for three months, keeping his head down in town, and he hadn't come into Hurley's for takeout once since he'd fired her. The man loved Hurley's po'boys and barbecue burgers and had a weakness for spicy sweet potato fries. That he hadn't stepped foot in Hurley's Homestyle Kitchen in three months was a clunk over the head of reality: he really wanted nothing to do with her anymore. He was here for the boys, she knew. Whether because they missed her or because he knew they'd love being in the holiday show or both.

He appeared in the doorway, all six feet plus of him, his handsome face showing no emotion. He tipped his dark brown Stetson at her. "Looks like you're packing up," he said. "We're too late?"

"We can't dishen?" Henry said, poking his blond head in and looking up at his uncle. He turned his attention to Clementine. "Hi, Clementine!"

Clementine smiled at the twins. "Hi, Henry. It's so nice to see you. Hi, Harry. And of course you can both audition."

"You're one of the only people who can tell the boys apart," Logan said. "And thank you. I'd hate if they missed out because of me. We got so busy decorating the tree in the barn and when I remembered the audition, I drove them into town as fast as I could without speeding."

What happened back in August? she wanted to shout. *Why did you shut me out?* She tried not to look at Logan, but his blue eyes drew her, as did the way his thick dark hair brushed the collar of his brown leather jacket. How could she still be so in love with a man who wanted nothing to do with her?

"No problem," she said, turning her attention to the

twins. "Do you boys know the song 'Jingle Bells'?" Kids under five only had to sing the chorus for their audition since the tryout was really just to see who could take on the speaking roles.

"Jingle bells," Henry sang.

"Jingle all the way," Harry added.

"Oh fun one a sleigh," Henry sang.

"A!" Harry ended with flourish.

Clementine suppressed her laugh. She wanted to scoop up those adorable Grainger twins and smother them with hugs and kisses. She hated the boundary Logan's very presence demanded. She glanced at the cowboy, moved by the utter love she saw in his expression for his nephews. He adored the boys and that was the most important thing. Not whether she was in their lives.

"You know what, guys?" she said to them. "You did great. You are both in the holiday show!" No matter how the littlest kids did on their "dishens," they were in the show, even if they couldn't get through the word *jingle*.

They ran over to Clementine and hugged her. She'd missed the feel of their sweet little arms around her so much. From last April to August, she'd spent just about every day with them between her lunch and dinner shifts, picking them up from their preschool program, taking them to the library, to the smoothie shop for their favorite concoctions, to Hurley's for the kids' mac and cheese that they loved so much. And she'd bring them home, so aware of their uncle Logan with every step in his house, his jackets and cowboy hats on pegs just inside the front door, the big brown leather couch he'd cuddle up on with the boys as he read to them. She'd give the twins a bath and bring them downstairs all ready for dinner, and sometimes he'd invite her to stay and she would—and she'd fantasize that he was her husband, these were her boys.

And then finally, the kiss. That amazing kiss. *He is attracted to me,* she'd thought. *I'm not crazy. Something has been building here.*

Until it crumbled along with her heart.

She could feel Logan watching her now and she snapped back to attention. The boys had run over to the play area, a big square with a colorful rubber mat set up with toys, blocks and books, and Logan was stepping close to her.

"Thank you," he said. "Being in the show means a lot to them."

They mean a lot to me, she wanted to say. *I miss them. I miss you. I miss what we had, what we started to have.*

"Rehearsals start tomorrow," she told him, forcing herself to be all business. "3:30 to 5:30. Monday, Wednesday and Friday will be the regular schedule. Louisa is helping out, plus I'm putting out the call for volunteers tomorrow, so the twins and other little ones will be in good hands."

He nodded. "I'll make sure they're there." He was looking everywhere but at her. "Boys," he called over, "let's get home for that ice cream I promised you."

As they walked out, each holding one of Logan's hands, that empty feeling came crawling back. What she would give to be with Logan and the boys in his living room, laughing over something silly and eating ice cream.

How was she going to handle seeing Logan Grainger six times a week for five seconds a time?

By shutting him out yourself, she realized. She'd tried over the past three months and for the most part, she stopped thinking about him so much. That was possible only because he'd made himself so darn scarce. But now that he'd be around so often, even for just drop-off and pickup, she wasn't sure her heart could take it.

She had to focus on all that was going on in her life and forget Logan Grainger. She had the play, her job, her family, her volunteer work, her side job and the call she was expecting any day now from the Texas Department of Family and Protective Services.

Logan Grainger, I am hereby quitting you. Quitting dreaming of you, thinking of you and hoping for something you've made clear will never be.

Thing was, it drove her insane not to know why he'd shut her out. And until she knew why, she would wonder and speculate what she'd done wrong, *if* she'd done something wrong. Something she did or said? Something in the letter he'd gotten that had made him fire her? What? What could possibly be the connection?

As she stood in the empty community center room, just her and a bunch of chairs, she made a decision about Logan Grainger, one she could live with.

She was going to find out why he'd fired her, why he'd dumped her the way he had. He owed her an explanation; yes, he did. She'd get her long overdue explanation and be able to put Logan Grainer to rest in her mind.

Not in her heart, not for a long time, but it was a start.

Chapter Two

The first thing Logan had thought of when he woke up in the morning was Clementine Hurley. For the past three months he'd put her out of his head, easily done with the dulled anger that had taken over his waking moments since he'd gotten Parsons's letter. Except when it came to Harry and Henry. From the time he got the boys up for breakfast and then ready for school, he was good Uncle Logan who put their needs first. But the second they were safely ensconced somewhere else, whether at school or with their sitter, the long-simmering burn would start churning in his stomach, thrumming in his head, questions with no answers.

This morning, though, his first waking thought had been Clementine and the questions he clearly saw in her eyes. She deserved better than how he'd treated her. But he didn't want to explain anything. He didn't want to talk. He just wanted to be left the hell alone.

Now, after dropping off the boys at school, Logan stood in the barn, grinding feed for the cattle, his own burning questions back full force. Was he this Clyde Parsons's son or not? Why would the man make up a lie and send a deathbed confession? Why would he stuff a safe-deposit box full of money for eighteen years and send Logan the key if he wasn't Logan's biological father?

Maybe Clyde Parsons had a mental condition and didn't know what he was doing. Maybe it was all one big mistake. His biological son was a *different* Logan Grainger. Once, someone had dropped off an unfamiliar wallet in Logan's mailbox with a sticky note on it: *Logan, found this by the steak house,* but the driver's license was for Logan *Granger* out in Grassville, a few towns over. Whoever had found it probably just quickly eyeballed the name, thought it was Logan Grainger's and dropped it off without noticing the Grassville address.

Yes, Clyde Parsons was probably Logan *Granger's* biological father. He'd just messed up the spelling of the last name. *Sorry, Logan Granger, but you've got a biological father out there you never knew about. Believe me, I know how you're going to feel when I straighten out this mess and discover it's you Parsons meant to send his deathbed confession to.*

Except Parsons had revealed some personal details in the letter. There was no way Logan Granger's father's name was also Haywood. Daniel, Peter, George, Tyler—sure, maybe. Haywood—no damned way.

For months Logan had been doing this, his mind

wrapping around any slight idea that would make the letter not true. But then the "oh yeah" would hit him a second later. Something that would send shivers up his spine to make him realize Parsons was probably telling the truth.

Logan was holding on to *probably* instead of definitely as long as he could.

What the hell had happened back then—twenty-eight years ago? His parents' wedding anniversary was eight months and three weeks before he was born. Logan never really thought about that much before, but the past three months, as logistics whirled around his head during barn chores or late at night in bed, he figured he'd come into the world a few weeks early. His brother had been five weeks premature and healthy as can be. So maybe Logan had been a couple of weeks premature too. If Parsons was Logan's biological father, then his parents had gotten married immediately after his mother had discovered she was pregnant. His mom and dad had both grown up in Blue Gulch, had known each other the way everyone does in a small town, but they'd never dated in high school until they'd suddenly married the summer after. So they'd had a whirlwind romance and gotten married. Happened all the time.

If it *was* true, had Haywood Grainger known? It was clear from Parsons's letter that his mother knew Clyde T. Parsons was the father of her baby. Had she told Haywood? Had his dad raised another man's child thinking Logan was his own flesh and blood?

Logan stopped grinding the feed and the silence was too much. He needed distraction. He needed to find out the truth, have his questions answered, but he wanted the truth to be that Haywood Grainger was his biological dad, that Parsons was lying or suffering from dementia and lost in an old dream of the girl who'd gotten away.

It was possible.

Logan adjusted his Stetson and stalked over to the far pasture, zipping up his leather jacket as the December first wind snaked around him. He looked out at the herd grazing, just watched them standing there, calm and steady. As always, the land, the herd, the ranch worked their magic on his head and heart and he felt better. The letter receded from his thoughts as he decided to move the herd out farther tomorrow and tried to focus on whether he wanted to take on Wildman, another old rodeo bull who needed to be nursed back to health. Logan had done that once when he first quit the rodeo, but it was lot of work and took time and Logan had little room for either.

His cell phone buzzed with a text. He grabbed it, worried as always that it had to do with the twins, that something had happened.

But it was Clementine.

I'll drop the boys off after the show rehearsal. I need to talk to you.—Clementine.

No question mark. Not "can" I drop off the boys. Not "can" we talk.

I will. I need. End of story.

Didn't she know it was too hard on him to see her? That she was the first woman who'd interested him since

The Liar? Plus, even more so, just the sight of Clementine reminded him of who he'd been before he'd gotten Parsons's letter: a Grainger. His father's son. Exactly who he thought he was. Albeit hardheaded and stubborn, fine. But his father's son. Clementine had been there when he'd gotten the letter. Hell, she'd brought it in from the mailbox, not that that was her fault.

In her presence, his life had completely changed. Went from one thing to another.

Maybe. If. He closed his eyes and shook his head, driving himself crazy. Something had to give here. He had to look up the guy or ask someone or find out something, dammit.

In the meantime, he could text Clementine back a *No, that won't work for me, I'll pick them up, no time to talk, bye.* He'd done that the first month after he'd pushed her out of his life. She'd show up at the house, she'd call, she'd text, and he just cruelly shut her out. He released a deep breath, another gust of cool wind going straight to his bones. Maybe by "I need to talk" she meant she wanted to talk about the twins and how often he should work with Harry and Henry at home on the songs they had to learn for the Christmas show.

Right.

This was his mind wrapping around stupid maybes when Logan wasn't a stupid man.

Clementine wanted to talk about *them*. About what happened last August. About why he'd closed the curtain on them before it had even gone up.

But he didn't want to talk about it with anyone.

Thing was, Clementine Hurley knew what it was like

to have a birth parent and be raised by someone else. Maybe talking to her would help him sort out some of the wild feelings that were making him crazy.

He shook his head. He'd talk to her, then he'd feel close to her again, then he'd be kissing her and suddenly he'd be losing his head again in a romance. He liked Clementine—truth be told, he more than liked her in a deep down way he never would allow himself to think too much about. But everything inside him felt like it was made of the same thing his hard head was made out of. Something had closed inside him, period. He was done with women, done with love and romance and thinking about marriage and the future. And as attracted as he was to Clementine, he wasn't about to use her for sex. He'd hurt her enough.

But maybe if he finally said something, gave her an explanation without going into specifics, just some general: *Got some strange news I don't want to talk about and can't deal with, so I'm laying low these days* kind of thing. A person on the receiving end of that explanation would have to respect that, right? She'd back off. He could go on trying his damnedest to pretend she didn't exist.

That settled, he texted back an Okay.—L and went back to the house to fill up a thermos with strong coffee, surprised to see his answering machine blinking on the house landline. Everyone who needed to get in touch with him had his cell phone number.

He pressed Play and headed to the refrigerator for the pitcher of iced tea the twins' sitter had made yesterday.

"I'm calling for Logan Grainger," a stranger's voice

said. "I'm from the Tuckerville Post Office. You have been noted on a form here as the emergency contact for the late Clyde Parsons. His PO box hasn't been paid in two months and will need to be cleaned out by the end of the week or the contents will be turned over to the state."

Logan froze. Emergency contact? How dare—

Logan counted to five in his head to calm himself down, then shoved the pitcher of iced tea back in the fridge, his mind on the key and the money Parsons had written about. Child support. Well, Logan didn't want anything to do with Parsons's money or his damned guilt. He hated the final paragraph of Parsons's letter and had almost ripped the thing to shreds right after he'd read it.

You'll also find some photographs in the PO box. There's one of your mama. To this day I swear she's the most beautiful woman I've ever seen. There's one of us together too that always killed me to look at. I screwed up big. I failed her and you. I just want you to know, most of all, that I'm sorry. I tried not to think of you and did a damned good job of it too. But now that I'm dying, I'm thinking about you a lot.
—Yours, Clyde Parsons.

My father is Haywood Grainger, you stinking liar, Logan wanted to scream. His father had been a great dad. He practiced soccer with Logan and Seth for hours in the fields. He'd chaperoned overnights in the woods for Boy Scouts. He'd patiently tutored Logan in chemistry, having to study the textbook himself first to understand it. He'd taught Logan to be proud of the small bit of land they owned, how to raise and care for cattle, how to ride a horse. He'd been the best father and had always made Logan feel okay about himself.

Because he didn't know he wasn't Logan's biological father? If he had known, would he have treated Logan differently? Or not? Had Haywood Grainger known or not?

More than anything else on earth at the moment, Logan wanted Parsons to be wrong. He wanted Parsons to have been mixed up. Or that the pregnancy and himself as a father was some fantasy he'd cooked up because his girlfriend, Logan's mother, had dumped him for a better man—Logan's father. Maybe Parsons really wasn't his biological father at all. Logan liked that train of thought.

Except there were pictures in the PO box. Not that they'd prove anything, but Logan could see what Parsons looked like. If Logan looked nothing like him either, then maybe he could go on forgetting the whole thing. Pretend he'd never gotten the letter, force it from his mind.

But since the seed of doubt was there, that he wasn't the son of Parsons, maybe seeing a photograph of Parsons would settle something for Logan either way. Or not. Now he was thinking in circles. Logan was surprised he hadn't collapsed in a dizzy heap on the kitchen floor.

That's it, he thought. *Just do it. Get it over with.* He grabbed the letter from where he'd stuck it between the side of the microwave and the wall, took out the little gold key and shoved it in his pocket. Then he put on his leather jacket and his Stetson, let his ranch hand know he'd be gone for a few hours, and headed for his pickup.

Tuckerville was just over an hour away. During the drive, he kept the radio loud to drown out his thoughts. When he pulled into the Tuckerville post office parking lot, he didn't hesitate; he got out of the truck and went inside, ready to finally do this, to know something for sure.

He fished the old gold key from his pocket. 137 was imprinted at the top of the key. He found the right box on the last row, stuck in the key and felt his stomach twist with the lock.

He opened the little square door. Inside the long, narrow box was stacks of money, small bills haphazardly bundled in rubber bands and a bunch of envelopes, some large manila ones, some letter size.

Logan pulled out the large envelope and reached in. He could feel several photographs.

He pulled one out. Ellie McCall Grainger sat on the bank of a river in one, grinning in the sunshine. She wore a yellow T-shirt and jeans rolled up to the knees, her bare feet in the water. God, he missed her. His mother was kind and patient.

He didn't have to wonder who had taken the picture.

He turned the picture over. *Beauty at the River.* With a date, November, twenty-eight years ago.

Logan was born almost exactly nine months later.

The next three photographs were also of his mother alone, smiling, looking very happy, either at the riverbank or in two of the photos at a farm stand, pointing at the display of Christmas wreaths.

He pulled out the final photograph and gasped, the picture slipping out of his hands. Logan stepped back, his hands shaking. No. No way.

Get ahold of yourself, he ordered.

He steeled himself and picked up the photograph, forcing himself to look at the man pictured, his arm around Logan's mother.

Clyde Parsons was a dead ringer for Logan. The height. The dark hair. The Clint Eastwood squint. The shape of his face, his features, the expression.

His stomach felt like someone had just socked him hard, and his head felt so woozy he had to grip the side of the box unit to steady himself.

Clyde Parsons had been telling the damned truth. Logan wasn't a Grainger.

Well, it was a good thing Clementine had gotten bold and insisted on bringing the boys home since Logan had arranged for her replacement, the twins' sitter, to drop them off at the rehearsal after school today. She had no doubt the woman would have come to pick them up too. Anything so that Logan could avoid her. Well, no more.

He didn't have to want to date her. But he couldn't just fire her without a reason. Dump her from his life with no cause. And she wasn't leaving tonight until she had that reason. She was tired of racking her brain at night, tired of wondering if she'd done something wrong. Tired of trying to figure out what in the heck was in that letter that seemed to change everything. And if she was going to spend the next few weeks with the Grainger twins at rehearsal, she had to know what had caused Logan to push her away.

She pulled up to the sprawling white farmhouse, the front porch festooned with white lights, a three-foot tall painted wood nutcracker soldier standing aside the door next to two sorry-looking carved jack-o'-lanterns that Logan probably couldn't bear to get rid of. Clementine loved how he tried so hard to make a sweet life for his nephews. Decorating for the holidays and carving pumpkins hadn't been part of his world before he'd taken them in. Last summer, he'd told her stories about his life on the rodeo circuit, and though it sounded lonely to Clementine, he'd said he loved it. He'd muttered under his breath about something, a bad incident, but he wouldn't talk about it. Then, Clementine had just been starting to understand Logan Grainger somewhat—he didn't like to talk about what upset him, same as her, same as probably lots of people, except her two sisters. Now she wished he was more like Annabel and Georgia and said outright what was digging at him.

Clementine turned around and glanced at the twins in the back in their car seats. Both of them were fast asleep, Henry's head hanging down, Harry's to the side, his little pink mouth open. Both clutched the little stuffed reindeers she'd bought for them from a sidewalk fund raiser in town. She couldn't bear to wake them.

Clementine walked up the three steps to the porch and smiled at the jack-o'-lantern, took a deep breath and knocked. Logan opened the door, eyebrow raised since his nephews weren't at her side. "The boys fell asleep in their car seats. I think the rehearsal tuckered them out. My gram brought turkey po'boys and a few side dishes as a surprise for everyone for the first rehearsal, so they did eat."

He looked past her at the car. "That was nice of her. Tell her thank you from me. I'll carry them up to bed."

She stood on the porch while he carried in Harry. When he went back out for Henry, she headed into the kitchen. She didn't work for Logan anymore and had no business going into his kitchen and making a pot of coffee the way she used to, but too bad. The man needed coffee and so did she. And she wasn't leaving without knowing what had him so tied up in knots.

He hadn't opened up to her in three months. Why would he now?

She heard him walking upstairs, then a door being slowly closed. Then his footsteps on the stairs again.

He came into the kitchen, glancing briefly at her. "Is that coffee I smell?"

"I took the liberty. You looked like you could use some." She bit her lip. *Well, go ahead, Clem. He's not going to bring it up.* "Logan, I—I know you've made it crystal clear that you don't want anything to do with me. I don't know what happened back in August. You kissed me, and I thought something was happening between us. Then a minute later, you read a letter and that was it. All of a sudden, the next day you fired me and wouldn't talk to me."

He turned away for a moment, then leaned against the counter, crossing his arms over his chest. "I'm sorry, Clementine. I was a real jerk to you."

But why? she wanted to scream. *Why, why, why?*

She waited for him to elaborate. Maybe if she stopped trying to fill the silence, he'd go on.

She could hear the coffee dripping into the pot. The second hand on the big analog clock on the wall ticking away. Her own beating heart.

He looked at her for a long few seconds, then said, "Can I ask you a personal question?"

Please do, she thought.

"Sure," she said, practically holding her breath.

He looked at her, his blue eyes intense, then he glanced away. "Did you feel, deep down, that the Hurleys were your parents, that you were their child? Or did you feel…adopted?"

What the heck? Where was this coming from? Was he worried about how the twins would feel being raised by their uncle?

She stared at him, having no idea where he was going with this or what this had to do with her question. But clearly, it did. "To be honest, both," she said. "But the Hurleys took me in when I was eight. From that point on, I did feel they were my parents and I loved them and I believed they loved me. Annabel and Georgia felt like my sisters from the start because they were so loving to me. They made me feel like I was one of them. But maybe because I *was* eight when they adopted me, I was very aware that for the years prior, I was in limbo. Foster care. I had a birth mother, but she couldn't take care of me."

He nodded. "Couldn't or wouldn't?"

Again, what the hell? Hadn't she and Logan talked

about this a bit when he'd first hired her as the boys' after-school sitter? He knew Clementine's story. It had come up because when she'd first starting babysitting for him last spring, not long after he'd come home to raise the boys, he once asked aloud if the twins would accept Logan as a father figure. She'd talked a lot about love and commitment and being there as what mattered.

"My mother was a drug addict," she said. "She had me at eighteen and managed to be clean during her pregnancy for my sake. That tells me a lot about her. She tried hard. But she couldn't stay clean and she was in and out of rehab for years. So I say *couldn't*."

"Well, sometimes it's about *wouldn't*."

She walked over to him and put her hand on his arm. He stiffened. "Logan, what is this about?"

He reached over to the counter to a few manila envelopes with a letter lying on top. He handed her the letter, which was from a Clyde T. Parsons in Tuckerville. "Read it," he said.

She gasped at the first sentence. Then about three more times. *Oh, Logan,* she thought. *What a thing to find out at age twenty-eight—and when everyone involved was gone.*

"This is about *wouldn't*," he said. He opened a cabinet and pulled out two mugs, then filled them with coffee and got out the cream and sugar.

She put the letter down on the counter and reached for her mug. "Not necessarily."

"Not necessarily?" he repeated, frowning. "He walked out on a pregnant woman. Walked out on his responsibilities to her and to me. Then he needs to die in peace so he flings a grenade at me as a parting gift? *Wouldn't*, Clementine."

Her heart constricted. This was complicated and messy and was tearing him apart, rightfully so.

She wrapped her hands around the steaming mug. "I'm just saying that there's a fine line between can't and won't. Sometimes people can't step up. They don't have it in them."

"Bull. I stepped up. My brother and his wife died leaving two little boys confused about why their parents weren't here anymore."

"You had it in you, Logan. You're strong. You care. Some people just can't handle things. So they walk away."

He shook his head. "You mean they won't, so they walk away. Anyone can step up."

Clementine felt lead weights on her shoulders. "I don't know." She really didn't. Her birth mother hadn't been able to, even thought she'd claimed quite a few times over the years that she *wanted* to. Sometimes, to keep your heart intact, you had to believe what you needed to believe. Clementine needed to believe in couldn't, not wouldn't.

Logan's jaw was set hard. "So you condone what Parsons did."

"No. Of course not. I'm just saying he very likely didn't have it in him to do anything else."

"I don't want to talk about this anymore." He turned away and took a long drink of his coffee.

She hadn't meant to shut him down. Maybe she was supposed to listen more, talk less?

If she didn't believe in her heart that her birth mother was a *couldn't* and not a *wouldn't*, Clementine was sure her heart would break in a thousand pieces. Sometimes, when she thought about Lacey Woolen, it was the only thing that kept Clementine okay.

"I can only talk about my particular situation and how I feel about it," she said. "I completely understand how you feel, Logan. The parting gift, the walking away, the grenade, I get it. God, what a bombshell."

"Why didn't my parents tell me?" he asked quietly. "How could they let me live a lie?"

"Probably because deep down and no matter what, you were Haywood Grainger's son, and that was no lie. It was their truth, Logan."

"But not *the* truth," he said, shaking his head again.

She wanted to go over and wrap her arms around him, but she didn't dare. "It's complicated."

He took another sip of his coffee. "Let's change the subject. How'd the boys do tonight?"

She smiled. "Great. They now can sing the first line of 'Jingle Bells' without a hitch. And that's only after one night of rehearsal."

"Isn't the first line just 'Jingle Bells' twice?"

She laughed. "Yes. But they're only three years old."

"They've missed you. I'm glad they can spend time with you."

She was quiet for a moment, then said, "At least I know now why you fired me, why you pushed me away. You were all torn up."

He nodded. "I'm sorry, Clementine. You deserved better than that."

So come over here. Kiss me again. Take me in your arms. Let me in now that I know. Maybe I can help.

He did none of the above. "I don't know who the hell I am," he added grimly. Am I even Harry's and Henry's uncle if I'm not a Grainger?" He shook his head. "That's dumb. Even if I'm just half, I'm still their uncle."

She put down her mug. "You are, no matter what."

"I hate this," he said. "I hate it all."

She bit her lip and let out a breath. "Have you verified that this Clyde T. Parsons is telling the truth? Have you seen the photographs he mentions in the letter?"

He explained about the call this afternoon, about the picture of Clyde Parsons being a dead ringer for him. He picked up one of the manila envelopes, reached in and pulled out a photograph of a man without looking at it, then handed it to her.

She took the photograph and stared at it. *Oh wow.* Clyde Parsons looked very much like Logan Grainger. They had the same features—except Clyde's eyes were hazel—the same hair, and there was something so similar in their expressions.

Her heart went out to Logan. How hard this must be. So much to take in, so many questions, no answers.

"Maybe Parsons has family," she said softly.

He shot a glance at her. "His family has nothing to do with me."

She wasn't so sure she agreed, but now wasn't the time to talk about that anyway. "I just mean that maybe you can find out who Clyde Parsons was, what he was like. You could do some poking around about him."

"Don't I know everything by his actions? He walked

out on his pregnant girlfriend. He let another man take responsibility." He set his mug down hard in the sink. "You know what? I'm done talking about this. Done thinking about it. Haywood Grainger was my father—he raised me. That's all I need to know."

Except the whole thing was tearing Logan apart. So it wasn't all he needed to know. It was what he *wanted* to know, but for closure, for peace, he'd have to do more than ignore the truth.

Clementine glanced at her watch. "Oh no, I'm late. My shift starts at six and you know how crazy busy Hurley's Homestyle Kitchen gets on a Friday night. "By the way, my sister Annabel told me that tomorrow's special is Gram's famed macaroni and cheese. Maybe you can bring the boys in for lunch. Oh and practice 'Jingle Bells' over breakfast."

He nodded. "Will do. And maybe we will come in for lunch tomorrow. I'd like to thank your grandmother for the po'boys. The twins love Hurley's po'boys."

And hadn't had them for the three months he'd been avoiding her, hung in the air between them.

"Logan, if you need to talk about this, you can call me or come see me anytime. You know that, right?"

"I'm done talking about it," he said, his blue eyes stony. "But…thanks," he added, his expression softening just a little.

She headed toward the door, wishing she could stay, wishing she could rush over to him and hug him tight. It took everything in her to walk to the door and leave him alone with his thoughts.

Chapter Three

Hurley's Homestyle Kitchen was open from 11:00 a.m. to 9:00 p.m. every day but Monday, and since Clementine was the head waitress, managed the waitstaff and helped in the kitchen between her shifts, she had little time to work on the Creole sauce she'd been trying to perfect for Hurley's special Christmas dinner menu. Hurley's wouldn't be open for usual business on December 24. Every Christmas Eve, Gram created a free buffet for those who might be alone for the holiday or unable to afford dinner.

Clementine loved her grandmother so much. The woman was always thinking about others, those who didn't have much money or family. At holiday time especially, she wanted Hurley's to be a place where people could come, alone or just hungry, and share in a special meal. Every year, Clementine invited her birth mother, who she knew lived alone in a one-bedroom apartment above the library down Blue Gulch Street and kept very much to herself. Every year, Lacey Woolen was noncommittal. Twice she'd shown up. Once, she peeked her head in, then quickly left, clearly uncomfortable. The other time, three years ago, she'd gotten as far as sitting down at a table with others but hadn't filled her plate and left after ten minutes.

Now, in the big country kitchen, Clementine yawned as she added chopped onions and garlic to the big pot for her Creole sauce. She'd spent a fitful night thinking of everything Logan had told her about the letter he'd received, the contents of the PO box and everything they'd talked about, including her birth mother. She'd thought Logan was a *wouldn't* all these heartbreaking months. But it turned out that he was a *couldn't*. Right now, Logan was dealing with the reality of having an answer to a question that had been tormenting him for three months. A man other than his beloved dad was his biological father.

Yes, right now, Logan was a *couldn't*.

As Clementine stirred her sauce, she wondered if Lacey would ever swing from *couldn't* to *could* and come to the Christmas buffet, if she'd finally give Clementine the one thing she wanted from Lacey: just the slightest, barest, most tenuous start of a relationship of some sort. They were two people with a fundamental connection, and since Clementine was a twenty-five-year-old adult, it seemed perfectly reasonable to Clementine that Lacey finally acknowledge that connection, open up in the slightest, share something about herself, anything, something. But she never had. It used to hurt Clementine terribly, in her bones. Now, it just drove her insane. *Come on, already, lady.*

"Um, Clementine? You're stirring your sauce kind of hard."

Clementine's hand stilled on the wooden spoon and she glanced up. Dylan Patterson, the eighteen-year-old line cook, was smiling gently at her.

"Don't all the best cooks, you included, Dylan, say you should put your emotion into your cooking?" Clementine asked.

"Not anxiety," her sister Annabel whispered with compassion in her voice as she passed by Clementine en route to the walk-in refrigerator. "Instead, you're supposed to tell your sister everything that's bugging you," she added with a commiserating smile.

"Sisters," Georgia said, nodding at Clementine from where she stood at the baking station. Even over the aroma of onions and peppers sautéing, Clementine could smell the first batch of biscuits baking. Georgia reached a floury hand to her belly. Her almost eight-months-pregnant belly. "That was some kick," she said laughing.

"I expect that little kicker to be one of my lead marchers in the holiday show in two years," Clementine said, hoping to keep the subject off herself and her mad stirring.

Georgia was due in late January. When Clementine thought her life was complicated she'd think back to what Georgia had gone through last spring and summer, first with an obsessed boyfriend who turned stalker then with a secret pregnancy—Detective Nick Slater's child. A good man who was now her husband. Georgia and Nick were responsible for bringing Dylan, their young cook, into Hurley's. Last summer they'd taken care of the then seventeen-year-old's newborn son for a week since he was afraid social services would come take his baby away. Clementine tried to remember that opening up was key, that keeping your troubles to yourself would make for stomachaches and awful sauces. But she had finally opened up to her sisters about Logan last summer and though talking about it had helped, nothing made her heart feel better. And now, how could she talk about her and Logan's conversation last night? That was his private business.

"Mine too," Annabel said, patting her own pregnant belly. Annabel was due in early March. The Hurleys were all beside themselves that another generation of Hurleys was on the way. "And Lucy is so excited to be in the show," Annabel added, carrying a carton of eggs back to her station where she was working on one of the Saturday lunch specials, ham and cheese frittatas. Annabel's stepdaughter, Lucy, was adorable and one of Clementine's most energetic singers.

Essie Hurley came into the kitchen and tied on her yellow apron. "Madelyn Parker just called. She's wants to hold her book club luncheon here at 12 noon. Better get another two cartons of eggs out, Annabel."

Saturday lunch at Hurley's Homestyle Kitchen was always busy. Clementine tasted her Creole sauce, declared it a B- and asked her Gram to try it.

"Clementine, it's delicious. Tiny bit more garlic next time, but absolutely great."

"Good to hear because my aunt is coming in for lunch today and she loves her spicy gumbo with Creole sauce," Dylan said as he dredged steak in flour for his amazing chicken-fried steak.

"So let's get to work!" Essie said.

With her sauce ready for the cooks, Clementine headed out into the dining room to check on the table settings and make sure the salt and pepper shakers and hot sauce jars were full. Despite working in this room since was a teenager, Clementine loved it. The wide-planked wood floors, the lemon yellow beadball walls with black-and-white photographs of Blue Gulch through the years and family photographs lining the doorway to the kitchen. The tables, some round, some square, were glass and each was decorated with an orange vase of wildflowers that Clementine picked every morning from the field beyond the backyard.

Clementine felt eyes on her and glanced out the window toward Blue Gulch Street. Lacey Woolen, her birth mother, stood there, foam cup of coffee in her hand. She wore her usual long skirt and cowboy boots, her long, graying dark hair in a braid down one shoulder. Lacey looked away when Clementine waved.

She wanted to march out there and shout, *What? What, what, what? Why do you come here practically every day to stare at me through the window, something you've been doing since I was eight years old? Why not say something? Why not come in and ask me to take a walk with you? Have lunch. Dinner. Anything. Some-*

thing. Lacey Woolen was so frustrating that Clementine wanted to scream.

"Maybe she'll come to Christmas dinner this year," Essie said from behind Clementine, her warm hands on Clementine's shoulders.

Clementine sighed. "I've given up on having expectations."

Her gram patted her shoulders and headed back into the kitchen.

Problem was, Clementine hadn't given up. She still had expectations. Hopes. She watched as Lacey turned to walk away, glancing at Clementine. They held each other's gazes for just a moment before Lacey continued walking.

The next time someone asked Clementine what she wanted for Christmas, she was going to say: the ability to read minds. Oh and not care so much what was on those minds.

At just after noon, Logan stood in the barn, tilting his head at the horses' Christmas tree. A laugh bubbled up inside him, but he squelched it back. He was surprised the tree, laden with every possible piece of tinsel and ornament, was still standing and hadn't toppled over from the weight.

"We're done!" Harry said, bits of tinsel in his blond hair. "Will the horses like it?"

Logan nodded and knelt down between the boys who stood admiring their tree. "I think they'll love it. In fact, why don't we lead Winnie out and see what she thinks." Winnie was a pony, a gift from West Montgomery, Cle-

mentine's brother-in-law and a fellow rancher. West had
given Logan the pony last spring after his brother's and
Mandy's funeral, and the twins adored the sweet speck-
led little horse meant to comfort them.

Logan opened Winnie's stall, the boys excited at his
side.

"Come on, Winnie. Look at your tree!" Harry said.

Logan led the brown-and-white pony out of the stall
and stopped a few feet from the tree. He smiled at the
homemade star both boys had worked on together. The
glitter on the coffee table was proof of their handiwork.

"What if she eats it?" Henry asked, looking up at
Logan. "What if she thinks the red stuff is apples?"

There was so much red tinsel wrapped around the
small tree that it was entirely possible Winnie would
mistake the tree for a giant apple and take a bite. But
she didn't. She stood there looking at.

"She likes it," Harry said. "I can tell."

"Me too," Henry agreed.

God, he loved these boys. Harry wore his Batman
cape, and Henry had some kind of big spy goggles atop
his head. Logan knelt back down and hugged them both
against them, keeping a hand on Winnie's lead. They'd
changed his life and kept him busier on all fronts than
he'd ever been in his life, but he loved them like crazy
and was grateful that they had each other. The twins
might be only three, but they'd taught him about a thing
or two about holding on and staying the course in the
face of grief and fear. He'd needed to be strong for
them instead of falling apart at the losses in his life,
the changes. Because of them, he'd stayed grounded.

He'd better start dealing with this thing about Parsons or it would eat him up inside. He had no room in his life for that. He had to be here and present for his nephews, especially now at Christmastime. At Thanksgiving dinner last week, just the three of them this year, they'd gone around the table saying what they were grateful for, and Harry had said he was grateful for his uncle Logan and the ponies, and Henry had said "me too." Logan had had to squeeze his eyes shut at the tears that had pricked.

"And I'm grateful for you wonderful boys, my Harry and my Henry," Logan had said.

"And for Crazy Joe?" Harry had asked, swiping a bite of turkey in gravy.

"And for Crazy Joe," Logan had said, glancing out the window and able to just make out Crazy Joe, an old rodeo bull, grazing in the far pasture.

He'd thought about that fifteen second conversation for days. Him. The twins. The ponies. Crazy Joe. It was so easy to be grateful for what was good and special in your life, what mattered most to you. He had to remember that, hold on to it. Three-year-olds magically kept his head level. He needed to keep that Thanksgiving conversation looping around his mind to stay with the here and now and stop letting this damned thing with Parsons take over his life and thoughts. He was the same person he was three months and a day ago.

Except, dammit, he wasn't. But he still had to figure out how to live with it, how not to let it consume him.

"Let's go wash up for lunch at Hurley's," he said, putting that train of circular thought out of his mind as he led the pony back to her stall. "I hear one of today's specials is the mac and cheese."

The boys zoomed out of the barn toward the house, Harry's Batman cape flying in Henry's face, which made him trip into Harry's path. Both ended up falling. Harry kicked at Henry; Henry kicked back at Harry.

"Dummy!" Harry shouted.

"Bigger dummy!" Henry yelled.

"Guys," Logan said. "How we'd go from being excited about going to Hurley's for mac and cheese to calling each other names?"

They shouted at each other for another ten seconds.

"Well, what are you going to do about this problem?" Logan asked, crossing his arms over his chest.

"Let's make up so we can have mac and cheese," Henry said to his brother.

"I'm getting lemonade with mine," Harry responded.

"I'm getting chocolate milk," Henry said as they both flew into the house.

Resolution. If only his own problems could be taken care of so simply and easily.

He followed the twins inside the house. "We have about a half hour before it's time to head over, so why don't you play a bit?"

The boys ran over to their blocks area and started stacking. Stacking and then running full speed into their block-walls was among their favorite pastimes.

Solution. Having a problem. Doing something about it. Right now his problem was that he was driving himself crazy and needed to know something more about Clyde Parsons than he did. Over the past few months he'd thought about people his mother might have confided in, but Ellie Grainger had always been so private that he couldn't imagine her telling such a personal thing to the few friends she'd had, such as their nearest neighbor at the ranch he'd grown up on, Delia Cooper, who was very chatty and social. His mother didn't have any siblings to open up to, either. She'd probably kept the information to herself.

Go over to the computer and type in Clyde T. Parsons and Tuckerville and see what comes up, he told himself.

Maybe he has family, he recalled Clementine saying.

That's of no concern to me, he recalled himself snapping back.

And it wasn't, he reminded himself. But he did have low-level basic curiosity about the man who'd fathered him. Did Parsons have siblings? Parents? Other children?

Not that they were any kin of his. Just because you shared DNA didn't make you family. Being there made you family. Giving a damn made you family. Taking responsibility made you family. But that DNA meant something in and of itself. Unfortunately. He shook his head at how danged complicated the whole thing was. Was, wasn't, wouldn't, couldn't, should, shouldn't, is, isn't. What the hell had happened to things being black or white? Gray areas were murky. Logan hated murky.

He forced himself over to the laptop computer on the living room desk and sat down. In the search bar, he typed in Clyde T. Parsons and Tuckerville, Texas, and hit Enter.

An obituary came up. A short obituary.

*Clyde T. Parsons, Tuckerville: Clyde Turnbull
Parsons was born on September 3, 1966 in Austin,
Texas, to Dotty and Delmont Parsons, who prede-
ceased him. A traveling man who supported himself as a ranch hand, Clyde lived all over the state
of Texas and spent the last two years in Tuckerville. A funeral is scheduled for Sunday, August
27 at three o'clock in the afternoon at the Tuckerville Funeral Home.*

No mention of leaving anyone behind. If he'd seen
his own name there he would be steaming mad, so at
least the man had had sense not to leave information
about Logan. But no other family?

So what, Logan thought. It wasn't as though he was
about to drive out to Tuckerville again and ask after
Clyde Parsons. What he'd been like. Why he'd spent
the last two years in Tuckerville. Logan had been to
Tuckerville a bunch of times over the past ten years.
Many rodeo events and the championships were held
in Stocktown, about fifteen minutes away, but Tuckerville had a bustling downtown where all the action was
afterward, particularly for champs, like he'd been until
The Liar had come along.

He shook his head to clear his mind of Bethany and
the rodeo and his life before this ranch.

*I don't care who Parsons was, why he couldn't stick
to one place, why he spent a couple of years in Tuckerville*, he told himself.

But dammit, a piece of him did. A piece of him
wanted to know something more.

"I'm starving, Uncle Logan," Henry said. "Is it time?"

Logan got up and headed over to where the boys were building a very high tower.

"How can we leave before you two knock over this wall? It's taller than you are."

The boys grinned, shot up and ran over to the far side of the room, then came hurtling over to the wall of blocks, one arm extended in a fist like a superhero, sending the blocks flying in every direction in a burst of laughter.

Logan smiled. Nothing like adorable three-year-old boys to take your mind off your troubles, even for just a minute.

Clementine took very good care of table four, the round one with the view of the mountain range in the distance and the handsomest men in the restaurant. The Grainger twins shared the special macaroni and cheese and smiley face fruit plate, and their uncle had the smothered chicken po'boy with a side of spicy sweet potato fries. As always, Clementine was touched by what a good father Logan was to his boys. He shushed them when they got too loud, he praised them for eating their mac and cheese with closed mouths, he made sure they knew that her sister Georgia's chocolate chip cookie dessert depended on not throwing a slimy piece of macaroni at one's twin brother—Henry—or shooting a grape off the table like a marble—Harry. Not for the first time she wondered how a man who'd lived and breathed for the rodeo circuit, no interest in settling down, had such fatherly instincts and patience. But Logan had both.

Back when she was babysitting for him over the spring and summer, he used to shrug and talk about what a great dad he'd had and how he probably just had a great firsthand teacher at fatherhood without even thinking much about it. Once he'd said he was probably more ready to settle down than he ever realized. Then he'd seemed to get all flustered at having said too much and retreated a bit, and Clementine knew that catching Logan Grainger might not be that easy, that she might have to wait to be caught herself. So she'd shaken off her expectations but kept her hopes, a hard balance, and then wham, a month later in August, the kiss. That beautiful kiss in the middle of his living room, his lips everything she'd fantasized about, along with what it was like to be in his arms, the object of his desire. Man, she'd been flipping happy in that moment.

When Clementine realized that Edwin Fingerman at table two had been trying to get her wandered attention, she snapped back to waitress mode and refreshed his basket of biscuits and apple butter. She noticed Annabel chatting with Logan and wondered what they were talking about. The smothered chicken po'boy probably. Annabel was an amazing cook.

She headed over to the Grainger table to clear plates and overheard the last bit.

"West and I are so glad they love their pony!" Annabel was saying. Clementine recalled that West had given the boys a pony when they'd lost their parents. He was a big believer in animal therapy. "So how about you pick up the boys from our ranch around six?"

What was this? Clementine stacked empty plates and raised an eyebrow at Annabel.

"I invited the Grainger boys over to the ranch for pony rides with Lucy and then a movie about horses," Annabel said. "Lucy keeps asking if the twins can come over and Logan said they'd love to. Plus the three of them can practice 'Jingle Bells' for you."

Clementine smiled. Truth be told, she felt a tiny bit left out, but she would get to see the Grainger boys three times a week now. Still, Annabel and West were on a friend level with Logan…and she wasn't.

"You're free for the afternoon," Annabel said to Logan. "Enjoy it."

"I guess it would be nice to have a few hours to myself," Logan said. "I appreciate it. Thank West for me too."

Annabel nodded. "Our pleasure. Oh, and Clementine, since there are three servers in the dining room, you should take a break yourself. Between working, volunteering at the foster home, directing the holiday pageant and spending all your spare time perfecting your Creole sauce, you deserve some time to relax. Go, shoo. I'll have Willa clear your tables."

Was Annabel Hurley Montgomery doing a little matchmaking here? Clementine narrowed her eyes at her sister and Annabel smiled. "Come on, boys," Annabel said to the twins. "I'll give you a tour of the kitchen and then we'll head over to my house to play with Lucy and ride the ponies."

"Yay!" the twins said in unison, leaping out of their seats.

"At least hug your uncle goodbye," Logan said, his arms outstretched. "I'll pick you two up at six. You be good for Miss Annabel, you hear?"

He got two nods, their blond mops shaking up and down before they zoomed into the kitchen with Annabel.

Clementine collected the cash Logan had left on the table, noting the hefty 50 percent tip he'd left.

"I'm good but not that good," she told him with a smile, then mentally kicked herself. She sounded like a flirty fool. The man was going through some serious life upheaval. And had made it clear romance between them was off the table.

He looked at her for a long moment. "I could use a sounding board, since you're free."

"Meet me on the porch swing in a minute," she said, curiosity building. Last night he'd shut down completely. Maybe he'd slept on what they'd talked about—about doing a little digging into his biological father's world.

Bless you, Annabel, she thought about her matchmaking sister as she made sure the dining room was indeed covered. Clementine would like to stay out on the porch and talk to Logan forever, really. She wasn't so sure *that* was in her best interest, but it was the truth.

"Remember last night when you mentioned that Parsons might have family?" Logan said as Clementine came out of the restaurant, two glasses of iced tea in her hands. He stood up and took one, waited for her to sit and then sat back down. "Turns out he didn't."

She was about to take a sip of her tea but paused. "He just died alone?"

Logan shrugged.

"Seems awful. No one coming to visit? No one to care?"

When she put it that way, he almost felt for the man—and was surprised he felt anything at all. "I guess some people don't want any entanglements, like to keep their lives small and closed. It makes me feel better in a way."

She tilted her head. "That he walked away from your mother because that's who he was?"

He glanced at her and nodded, grateful that he didn't have to answer a bunch of questions; Clementine just seemed to get it. "He probably wasn't capable of more, period. I guess you were right about the *couldn't*." He shrugged, shaking his head. "I don't know. It helps to think so."

She touched his arm. "Sorry about all this, Logan. I know it must be hard to take in."

He leaned his head back against the swing, staring at the white Christmas lights strung across the top. He pictured Clyde Parsons, an almost thirty-years-older version, lying in some hospice without a single visitor. No family. No friends. No neighbors.

Though that was what you got for being a class A jerk, Logan thought. *You died alone. With no one.*

Bitter much? he thought, again worried that he'd let that bitterness seep inside his bones and make him harder than he already was. The twins needed their guardian to be warm and fun-loving, not a brooder.

"Why do I have this notion to go to Tuckerville and find out something about him?" he said. "Why do I even care who he was?"

Clementine smiled at a couple walking up the porch steps to the restaurant. "It's natural," she said once they went inside.

"Doesn't feel natural at all. In fact, it feels very unnatural."

"Well, I do know what you mean. When I was a kid, I wanted information about my biological father, but the times I was physically close enough to my birth mother to ask, she'd pretend she couldn't hear me or she'd just change the subject to the weather. When I was eighteen, my caseworker finally gave me his name, which was on the record and I looked him up. I felt no connection at all to the person who'd come up in the search. That did feel unnatural—knowing you had someone's DNA, someone's blood coursing through your veins, yet they were just a name. So I do understand, Logan."

He glanced at her and nodded, part of him wanting to get up and walk away. Sometimes when he talked to Clementine, the intensity of it all was too much. The way she seemed to understand him, the way she looked at him, the way he wanted her. "Did you find out anything about him you would have been better off not knowing?"

She bit her lip and nodded. "He had a similar rap sheet to my mom's of drug arrests and he died of an overdose when I was five. The information didn't make me feel better, of course, but I was glad to have it. Sometimes you just have to know, especially when it concerns you in such a basic way."

Logan had the urge to draw Clementine against him. She spoke so matter-of-factly, but he knew somewhere deep inside all the harrowing things she'd been through, the pieces of her past, her history, had to rise up sometimes and poke at her. He was glad he'd opened up to her, something he never did since he didn't have anyone to open up to. Just the cattle and the horses. Not only was he able to talk to Clementine, she understood. Even if they didn't see eye to eye on everything, she *understood*.

"My birth mother was in and out of my life from the age of two," she said, taking a sip of her tea. "You know my story—then I was in a few different foster homes until I was eight and the Hurleys took me in. They were great parents. Everything a kid could ask for in a mother and a father. But being curious about my biological parents isn't a reflection on that. It's just natural curiosity. A man and a woman had a baby. That baby was me. That man and that woman are a part of my history. Of course it means something. So of course you want to know more about Clyde Parsons."

He'd been blindsided as an adult. He tried to imagine a tiny Clementine, confused and wondering where her mother was, why she didn't have a father, why she had to live with strangers in foster care. Again he was gripped by the urge to take her hand and hold it. *Shake it off, man*, he ordered himself. "I don't want it to mean something. I hate that it does."

"You've got the whole afternoon to yourself till six," she said. "You could drive out to Tuckerville right now and see if you can find out something, settle something for yourself."

"Maybe you—" Why the hell did he just say those words? Yeah, he couldn't imagine going to Tuckerville alone and asking about his biological father. But bringing Clementine further into all this wasn't a good idea. He wanted distance from her. Yet here he was, blabbing his innermost problems. And he almost asked her to come with him.

"Or I could come with you," she said, glancing at him.

He wished she wasn't so good at reading his mind. He wasn't about to start something up with Clementine or anyone. He'd done enough damage last summer. His insides felt shuttered, so completely closed he was sometimes surprised when his heart lurched over watching the twins sleep or some silly antic of theirs. Or when he looked at Clementine sometimes. Like when she'd come out on the porch with the glasses of iced tea in her Hurley's waitress uniform, which was a yellow apron that hid her sexy body. She had a heart-shaped face and round brown eyes and a wide pink mouth and that long, dark hair. He found her almost irresistible. But resist her, he would. So why ask her to come with him on the most personal journey of his life?

Because he couldn't go alone. He just couldn't. If he did end up talking to someone who'd known Parsons, who knew how he would feel? He might get all riled up or start shaking the way he did when he'd found out his brother and his wife had died. He'd been alone that day, grumbling mad about the bull besting him the night before at a rodeo, his attention still all over place since what happened with Bethany and how she'd betrayed him and cost him a championship the week before. So he'd been alone in a cheap motel room when he'd gotten the call from the Blue Gulch police. They'd gone to the ranch and had spoken to the sitter who'd led them to the kitchen and the list of emergency contacts. Logan was the first name.

He'd sat on that thin bed, trembling, unable to believe what he'd heard. Then he'd thought of the twins, just two years old then, innocently playing and with no idea that one conversation later, their entire world would change. He'd gotten up, quickly packed and headed to Blue Gulch in a state so numb he was surprised he'd gotten home alive. He'd had that conversation with the boys and he'd never looked back, the past, including the rodeo, Bethany, all of it, gone.

Now here was Parsons, forcing Logan's hand with a new past he hadn't even known existed. Hell yeah, Logan had no idea how he'd react to learning more about him, meeting someone who knew him.

He *needed* Clementine to come with him.

And he didn't like that one bit.

Chapter Four

Logan appreciated that Clementine was mostly quiet on the drive over, except to point out a beautiful tree and an old Italian restaurant where her grandparents had celebrated their engagement fifty years ago. Otherwise, she looked out the passenger window, humming along to the radio. She seemed to know he needed to be alone with his thoughts rather than voice them. The closer he got to Tuckerville, the more his stomach clenched. And not only because this was where Parsons had lived and died.

Logan hated Tuckerville. It reminded him of Bethany, since after the rodeo in nearby Stocktown they'd drive into Tuckerville and he'd take her out for a great steak dinner, then dancing, which he wasn't great at, and then he'd upgrade his hotel for her and they'd spend hours in bed.

She'd worked on him for two weeks, making him late for one rodeo because he'd been so consumed with lust. Okay, fine, he'd chalked that up to being a red-blooded male. But then she'd gone in for the kill and made him miss the championships in late July altogether and the potential of a huge purse. He knew he would have won that championship too.

He'd forced her faux angelic face and long blond hair out of his mind. Logan had never thought himself as particularly trusting or cynical, but he had no idea he could misread someone's intentions to the degree he'd misread The Liar.

Stop thinking about it, he told himself. *You've got bigger worries than a con-woman who tricked you.*

"I've never been here," Clementine said as she shut the car door and looked around. "Nice place. Busy. Much busier than Blue Gulch."

"I prefer Blue Gulch," he said. "Mile long main street, just the shops and businesses you need, neighbors who know everyone. I didn't even realize what a small-town guy I was until I moved back to raise the twins."

"I feel the same," Clementine said. "My sisters both left for big cities after high school but I never wanted to. I love Blue Gulch. It does have everything I need."

Another thing they had in common.

Downtown Tuckerville was bustling as usual on a Saturday afternoon, people running errands, going shopping, sitting at the outdoor restaurants even though it was barely sixty degrees today. On the corner was the steak house Bethany loved. He scowled at it and began walking to get away from it.

"I don't even know where to start," Logan said, stepping out of the way of a dogwalker with a big pack. "The obituary didn't offer much information. Just where and when he was born, his parents' names, the hospice where he died and the funeral home."

"Let's go to the hospice," Clementine said. "Maybe we can talk to his doctors and nurses."

"If they'll tell us anything," Logan said. He pulled up the obituary on his smartphone and noted the address. "We can walk. It's just a few blocks that way."

As they neared the three-story brick building with its flower-lined walkway, Logan was very aware of Clementine beside him. She'd taken off her apron and changed from her T-shirt and jeans into an off-white fuzzy sweater and gray pants. As much as he wanted distance between them, she felt familiar and comfortable, a help as they walked up the path to the door of the hospice—and all this unknown territory.

The receptionist had them wait for about five minutes, then a nurse's aide came to see them in the empty waiting area. In her forties, with assessing brown eyes behind red-framed eyeglasses and short dark hair, she sat in the padded chair across from them. Her name tag read Jennifer Cotter.

"You're here about Clyde Parsons?" she asked.

Logan nodded. "I'm...his biological son, Logan Grainger."

Talk about unnatural. Logan was pretty sure that was the strangest statement that had ever come out of his mouth.

He cleared his throat and shifted in his chair. He

gestured to Clementine. "This is Clementine Hurley." The two women smiled at each other, giving Logan a second to catch his breath. "I didn't know until a few months ago that he *was* my biological father," Logan added. "Did you know him well?"

The aide looked at Logan for a long moment, and he wondered if she knew about him, how much Clyde had told her. "Well, I was assigned to Mr. Parsons but he was here for less than two weeks before he passed away. He knew he was very ill but waited until he couldn't take care of himself or Phoebe before checking in here."

Logan glanced at Clementine, then back at the nurse. "Phoebe?" Logan pictured one of those little white fluffy dogs. Or maybe Phoebe was a cat.

"His stepdaughter," the aide said. "Ex-stepdaughter, I guess. Phoebe Pike. Phoebe came to see Clyde every day, even though her aunt thought it was morbid. That woman," she added under breath.

"Stepdaughter?" Logan repeated, glancing at Clementine again. "The obituary didn't say anything about a stepdaughter."

"Well, to be honest, Mr. Grainger, Clyde wrote out that obituary himself, said it was just as he wanted it. I asked him if he wanted to include Phoebe's name, but he said he didn't feel right about including one child and excluding another."

Logan was that other child, he figured.

"And since Phoebe wasn't a relation," the aide continued, "since she's his ex-wife's daughter, it didn't seem strange not to mention her by name or association, even though Clyde had been caring for her on his own for almost two years."

What the heck? An ex-stepdaughter? Two years? Where was the wife?

"How old is Phoebe?" Clementine asked.

"Nine, I think." The aide lowered her voice and leaned in. "Apparently a couple of years ago Clyde's wife left him to be a showgirl in Vegas, then got some quickie divorce and remarried and moved across the country. She just left the girl with Clyde. When he knew his time was coming, he found an aunt of Phoebe's about a half hour away who said she'd take Phoebe in if she couldn't track down the mother. The aunt had no luck with that, so Phoebe went to live with her."

Logan glanced at Clementine. The look in her eyes was a combination of concern, sadness and worry.

"That poor girl," Clementine said, shaking her head. "She must have been so confused about her place in this world."

The aide glanced at Clementine with commiseration. "Confused is right. And grief-stricken. Apparently she and Mr. Parsons were close. That girl came to see him every day. Apparently more than once she took the bus on her own since her aunt wouldn't drive her more than twice a week."

"Were you and Clyde close?" Clementine asked. "You seem to know so much about him and Phoebe."

Logan wasn't so sure he liked where Clementine was going with this. He was pretty sure she was heading for a question about what Clyde was like, what kind of man he was, if the aide liked him, or if he was a rotten bastard. Dying or not. He shifted his seat again, uncomfortable as hell, not sure he wanted to know any of this.

Yeah, they were here for information. But there was such a thing as too much information. Which he felt he already had. Parsons had been raising his ex-wife's nine-year-old stepdaughter? What? And the child of a woman who'd skipped out of him? Double what?

"We weren't close," the aide said. "Toward the very end, some patients do like to get some things off their chests. In his very final days, Mr. Parsons started talking about his life some. The girl's situation, how he picked a wife like himself who couldn't commit to anything. He did mention he had a son he never met. In fact, he asked me to mail a letter to you the day before he passed. He knew his time was coming. I sure was glad for him that he got it done beforehand."

Logan nodded. Part of him did want Clementine to ask what Parsons had been like. Nice guy? Ornery grump? Of course, he could just ask that question himself. But he couldn't bring himself to do so.

"How would you describe Mr. Parsons?" Clementine asked, practically on cue.

He glanced at her, again surprised by how she seemed able to know what he was thinking, that he'd gone from not wanting her to go there to the opposite.

"As I mentioned, I didn't know him well," the aide said. "He was easy to work with, treated me respectfully and kindly. He wasn't all that talkative, though he did talk a lot to the girl when she visited. I'd come in his room to check on him and they'd be talking away, the girl's chair pulled up along his bed. I got the feeling he was comforting her."

So not an obvious class A jerk. Or a grumpy coot. From what the aide said, Clyde Turnbull Parsons sounded like a decent person. Which was impossible. Decent people didn't walk out on their pregnant girlfriend without a backward glance. They just didn't.

Clementine was looking at him and she shifted in her chair, crossing her legs. She seemed to notice he was… uncomfortable. "So his stepdaughter—Phoebe—she's living with her aunt?" Clementine asked, and he was glad for the change in focus.

"Actually, I heard through the grapevine that that situation didn't work out too well," the woman said.

Clementine sat up straight. "Didn't work out too well? What do you mean?"

The aide leaned close again and lowered her voice. "Well, like I said, Mr. Parsons had arranged for the mother's sister to take Phoebe in, but there was some friction between her and the girl."

"Friction?" Clementine asked. "I guess they both had to get used to the new situation."

"Well, I heard through the grapevine that the aunt decided it wasn't working out," the aide said. "Phoebe's in a group foster home in Tuckerville now, the Tuckerville Children's Home, I think it's called. Or something like that."

Logan glanced at Clementine; she was shaking her head slightly, confusion in her expression.

"She's in a group foster home?" Clementine repeated. "After all she'd been through?"

The woman nodded. "The poor girl got dealt a hard hand." She glanced at her watch. "I'd better get back to work. I'm very sorry for your loss, Mr. Grainger."

Logan's chest felt tight and he nodded. "Thanks for the information."

They both watched the aide walk back down the hall. Logan's head was about to explode.

"Maybe we could go check on Phoebe," Clementine said. "Make sure she's all right."

Logan stared at her. No. There would be no checking on Phoebe. He'd come to Tuckerville. He'd gotten his information. He knew more than he had a couple of hours ago and wouldn't mind some time to let it all sit. "She's of no relation to me. She's not even a blood relation of Parsons."

Clementine stood up. "All I know is that my heart is breaking at the thought of a nine-year-old being tossed around like that. She lost her stepfather, the only person who was willing to care for her despite being an *ex*-stepfather. Her mother walked out on her and is nowhere to be found. Her aunt didn't want her, apparently. And Logan, it's coming on Christmas."

"I understand all that, Clementine. But the girl is no concern of mine. Or yours."

But even as the words came out of his mouth, he pictured a grieving, confused, disillusioned girl sitting in an unfamiliar house, wondering what had happened to her life.

Logan knew what that was like.

"If we could just make sure she's all right," Clementine said, biting her lip. "Logan, I can't leave Tuckerville without knowing."

He let out a deep breath and stared down at the floor for a moment. "And what if she's not? Then what? She's not my family, Clementine."

She wrapped her arms around herself and walked over to the window, staring out. "I just want to check on her."

He closed his eyes for a second, then surprised himself by walking up behind her and taking her hand. She turned around and looked up at him. "We'll just make sure she's all right, then we'll leave. A short visit."

Her shoulders slumped with relief as her entire face brightened.

He didn't like *how* he'd made her happier, but he was glad for it anyway.

The Tuckerville Children's Home was located in a nice enough ranch-style house with a big backyard. A woman and three kids, two boys around five and a girl of maybe thirteen, sat on the porch, making origami snowflakes.

Clementine had volunteered at many group foster homes over the past several years, everything from helping the house mother with chores to leading a cooking class or trip to the library to listening to the kids' secrets and hopes and dreams and trying to have a soothing or uplifting response. She glanced up at the well-kept house, noted how the foster mother smiled at the boy as she helped him cut his snowflake, how one of the girls giggled in delight when she opened her origami. There was happiness here and Clementine breathed a sigh of relief.

Logan seemed frozen beside her, but then he cleared his throat and approached the porch. "Hello. I have a connection to Clyde Parsons, who was caring for Phoebe Pike before he passed away three months ago. My friend Clementine and I thought we'd see how she's doing."

The woman gave a slight shake of her head and came down the steps. "That girl is impossible," she whispered, glancing back at the kids on the porch as if to make sure they weren't listening. "Wants nothing to do with anyone or anything. I've washed my hands. I've already told the caseworker it would be in her best interest to be moved. When she does bother to talk to the other kids, she upsets them with her negative attitude and stories. I can't have that."

Shunted again, Clementine thought. She knew what that was like. She glanced at Logan, his expression unreadable.

"Phoebe, you have company," the woman called toward the house.

"Not interested," a girl's voice called back.

But a face came to a window on the second floor. A cute girl wearing a backward baseball cap. Straight sandy-brown hair fell to her shoulders.

Phoebe glanced at Clementine with a bored expression, then at Logan. Suddenly the girl's eyes opened wide and her mouth dropped open. She rushed away from the window.

In a whirl, the girl was downstairs, racing over to them. She wore a Texas Rangers T-shirt, jeans and red sneakers with rainbow laces. "Logan Grainger? It's you, isn't it? Logan Grainger. I don't believe it."

"You know me?" Logan asked and Clementine wondered if Parsons told the girl he had a son he'd never met.

Phoebe's big hazel eyes widened. "Do I *know* you?" She laughed. "You're a three-time bull riding champion. I can't believe you're standing right in front of me. My… Clyde, my stepfather, he's gone now, but he took me to all your events. I guess you were his favorite too. He kept a scrapbook of all your events and championships. I have it now."

Clementine looked at Logan. The man looked absolutely gobsmacked, as though he had too much information clunked on his head at once.

"So what are you doing here?" Phoebe asked. "Did I win the contest?"

Logan glanced at Clementine with the same question in his eyes that she had swirling in her head. *What contest?*

"Lunch with your favorite bull rider, right?" Phoebe asked. "Clyde helped me enter months ago, but then he died and if I won, I was gone by then, living with my aunt. But that didn't work out, so now I'm here."

Logan seemed to let it all sink in for a moment. "You know what?" he said. "You *did* win the contest. Lunch with Logan Grainger. If it's all right with you, ma'am," he said to the house mother. "I can see a restaurant on the corner where we can take her for lunch, if you'd be comfortable with that."

The woman looked confused for a second, as if trying to put together what Logan had said about having a "connection to Clyde Parsons" and now Phoebe winning a contest. Hopefully she wouldn't ask questions in front of the girl. "Sorry," she said. "You could be the governor and I couldn't allow it. You can order in lunch here, if you'd like, and have it in the backyard. Of course I'll be keeping an eye."

"That would be fine," Logan said.

"What's your favorite food?" Clementine asked Phoebe.

"Anything barbecue and Mexican," Phoebe said. "I love spicy chicken tacos."

"There's a Mexican place two blocks up," the woman said. "And they're fast."

Within a half hour, Logan and Clementine were back with a big bag of takeout that they set on the picnic table in the large backyard. Two spicy chicken tacos for Phoebe with a side of beans and rice, a black bean quesadilla for Clementine and a loaded beef burrito for Logan. He'd been quiet while they'd gone for the food and Clementine hadn't filled the silence with comments or questions. She could tell he needed to just let thing be, not get overwhelmed by her thoughts on top of his own.

Clementine dipped a tortilla chip into the delicious container of salsa. "So you went to a lot of Logan's rodeo events?" Clementine asked.

"Lots of 'em," Phoebe said. "The last time was right after they were calling you the Handcuff Cowboy. That was a long time ago, though. Clyde said he heard you had some family business and quit the rodeo."

Logan's set down his burrito and uncapped his soda, but didn't say anything.

"The Handcuff Cowboy?" Clementine asked, looking between Logan and Phoebe.

Logan sipped his drink and clearly wasn't going to answer the questioning look in her eyes. He had a *change the subject—now* look in his own eyes.

"I think because he had the bull all locked up," Phoebe said. "Something like that."

Clementine stole another glance at Logan. He picked up his burrito and took a big bite. Can't answer a question with a full mouth, that was for sure.

"So Clyde was your stepfather?" Logan finally asked.

She nodded. "Clyde and my mom were married less than a year. My mom left and said she'd send for me when she was settled in Las Vegas. She wanted to be a showgirl. I'm not sure if she made it or not. She called every couple of weeks, but always said it wasn't the right time for me to come live with her. She knew Clyde was a great stepdad, so she wasn't too worried about me."

"Was he?" Clementine couldn't help but ask. "A great stepdad." She felt Logan glaring at her for asking the question he might not be ready for the answer to.

"Clyde was awesome," Phoebe said. Her face fell. "I wish he was here."

"I'm so sorry for your loss, Phoebe," Clementine said. As she watched the girl pick up her lemonade, she could see the expressions changing in her eyes, trying to forget and compartmentalize and focus on where she was right now. Clementine remembered doing that often herself as a kid.

Phoebe bit into her second taco. "Clyde was my mom's third husband. The other two were nice like Clyde. My mom used to say Clyde didn't have much money but he was the best-looking man she'd ever seen so she couldn't resist marrying him." She rolled her eyes and took another bite of her taco.

Clementine felt a warm hand rub her back for a moment, and she glanced at Logan, surprised he'd picked up on her need for a soothing gesture.

"So then you went to live with your mom's sister?" Logan asked.

Phoebe nodded. "Aunt Carol. When Clyde was in hospice, he told me he'd arranged for me to live with her, that everything would be great, that I'd have a mom figure in my life again. But Aunt Carol wasn't anything like Clyde. She can't stand noise or mess and I guess she wasn't ever close with my mom, either. We had terrible fights. Aunt Carol tried to get in touch with my mom but couldn't and one day a social worker came to get me. That's how I ended up at the foster home. But Mrs. Nivens doesn't like me either. I don't really care, though. Once my mom finds out that Clyde died, she'll come for me. I know it. Christmas Eve, I'm sure of it."

Clementine's heart squeezed in her chest. This girl seemed to be setting herself up for heartbreak. And she'd been through enough.

"When's the last time you talked to your mom, Phoebe?" Clementine asked, hating to put the question on the table.

Phoebe bit her lip. "Two years ago. She called on Christmas Eve and said she was getting married and moving overseas somewhere and that I should always remember she loves me." She smiled, but the smile faltered a few second later. "But she never called again and no one knows how to get in touch with her."

Oh, Phoebe, Clementine thought, her heart busting out of her chest for all this child had gone through.

"I thought nothing good would ever happen to me," Phoebe said. "But this is wild that I won the contest.

I can't believe I'm sitting here with Logan Grainger. I know you're retired and all, but you were my hero. I'm thinking about becoming a bronc rider when I'm older."

Logan's features softened. "You can do anything you set your mind to. That's what my father always told me. I believe it."

Phoebe finished her taco. "My teacher always says that. Mrs. Nivens too, but then she adds all kinds of ifs and buts that drive me insane. No matter how hard I study, I'm not getting an A in math. Or even a B."

Logan laughed. "I was never all that great at math either."

The girl grinned. They talked a bit about the rodeo, a world Clementine didn't know much about.

"Well," Logan said. "I guess we'd better get going." He stood up and started collecting empty wrappers and paper plates and stuffing them inside the take-out bag. "Looks like a nice place," he added, glancing at the big tree and the house.

Phoebe's face fell. "Yeah, real nice. Mrs. Nivens can't stand me. Whatever. At least I have this. I've never won anything before. This was really awesome, meeting you." She glanced at Clementine. "And you too," she said. "Are you married?"

Clementine felt her cheeks burn. "Just friends."

Phoebe tucked a swath of sandy-brown hair behind her ear. "Mr. Grainger, do you think I could have your autograph?"

Clementine could tell he was touched. He extended his hand toward Phoebe. She grabbed it with both of hers. "Of course. And call me Logan." He pulled a card out of his wallet, then leaned it against the wallet and scrawled his name in black ink on the back of it. "Here you go. I'm a rancher now in Blue Gulch. This card has my cell phone number on it. You can call me if you ever want to talk about the rodeo, okay?"

Clementine was so surprised by the kind gesture that she almost gasped. Not at the kindness; she knew Logan had a big heart, but at giving Phoebe access to him. No matter what he'd said about Phoebe being no concern of his, the girl's story had clearly gotten to him as it had Clementine.

Phoebe's eyes lit up and nodded. "Thanks. And thanks for the Mexican food. It was amazing."

They said goodbye, then waved at Mrs. Nivens, who was watching through the kitchen window. Clementine did like that the woman seemed careful with her kids. As Mrs. Nivens came out into the yard, Phoebe ran into the house clutching the card Logan had given her.

"Maybe meeting her big hero will give that girl an attitude change," Mrs. Nivens said, pursing her lips. "She tell you she wants to be a bronc rider someday? I'd say rodeo clown is where she's headed." She shook her head.

Clementine's stomach twisted at the criticism. She glanced up at the second-floor window, Phoebe standing there, waving, her expression wistful.

Logan held up a hand too and Phoebe smiled.

Then she and Logan headed back to his car, Clementine's heart heavier than ever.

11:48 p.m. Logan turned over in bed for the millionth time, unable to fall asleep. He'd tried, just so he could forget about today for a bunch of hours. Clyde had walked away from his pregnant girlfriend. Phoebe's mother had walked away from her. Phoebe's aunt had washed her hands of the girl. How the hell did people do that?

And why didn't this Clyde T. Parsons make any damned sense? Why would Parsons take such nice care of his run-off ex-wife's daughter? A home, sharing his love of the rodeo with her, giving her something to dream about.

To make amends somehow for mistakes he'd made when he was younger?

He punched his pillow, then got out of bed and paced the floor, then straightened his closet, which hadn't been that messy. He headed downstairs and cleaned the kitchen till the white porcelain shone, then went after the counters. In the living room he organized the twin's toys, then slammed over the blocks he'd just stacked, his frustration building.

What the hell was he supposed to do with all this... information? He didn't want Parsons to have been a decent person. He hadn't been. A decent person wouldn't have walked out on his pregnant girlfriend, he thought for the tenth time. End of story.

But he'd been decent to Phoebe, who wasn't even his blood. Someone's else's kid, and the daughter of a woman who'd run off on him and her own child.

He shook his head and restacked the blocks.

He heard his cell phone buzz with a text and went into the kitchen, where he'd left it on the shining counter.

Clementine.

Can I come over? I have to talk to you. Now.—C.

Oh hell. What was this about? He didn't want to know. He could just not text back. Act like he hadn't gotten the text.

He let out a breath and texted back, Everything okay?

I really need to talk. Now.

Okay, he typed back and dropped down on the chair at the kitchen table. He didn't want to speculate so he got up and made a pot of coffee and set out two scones from the box of goodies Clementine's sister had packed up for him and the twins when he'd picked up the boys from the Montgomery ranch earlier tonight.

Ten minutes later, he heard a gentle rap at the door and he let her in.

Clementine burst inside. "I can't stop thinking about Phoebe in that home with that woman who can't stand her. Granted, I'm sure her attitude and behavior has a lot to do with it. But, Logan, you're her hero. Think about what you can do for that girl. You can change her entire life."

Logan stared at her. "Are you saying you expect me to take her in?"

"Not you," she said. "I know you have your hands full. Me."

"You? *What?*"

She lifted her chin. "I'm a sign-off away from being certified to become a foster mother in the state of Texas. It's something I've been working toward these past few months. Gram and I even completed the home study two weeks ago. After my paperwork is signed off any day now, I'll be approved to be a foster mother. I want to take in Phoebe."

Logan stepped back. This was too much. Too damned much.

She stepped toward him. "She has no one, Logan. Just like I had no one until the Hurleys became my foster parents."

Logan turned around and stared out the window at the darkness. "I don't know how I feel about this." He could sense something beginning to shutter inside him, in his mind, in the region of his heart. He didn't want to be talking about this, thinking about it. What the hell? How did he go from bringing the boys to have the mac and cheese special at Hurley's for lunch to Clementine rushing over at midnight wanting to take in his biological father's ex-stepdaughter?

"She's a connection to you, Logan. Not in the most linear of ways, but a connection nonetheless. And you're her hero. I think the two of you can do a lot of good for each other. If I can foster her, perhaps she can spend some time at your ranch, learning the ropes a bit."

"How is she a connection to me?" he shouted, then closed his eyes and lowered his voice. "She's Parsons's stepkid. *Ex*-stepkid. And he's not my family, Clementine. He's just some man who got my mother pregnant and walked away. That doesn't make him connected to me. So she isn't either."

But even as he said the words, he knew they weren't true. There *was* a connection.

He shook his head, his stomach twisting. "I don't know, Clementine. I don't know about any of this."

She touched his arm and he flinched. "Think it over?"

He stared at her. "You going to foster her even if I say I don't want you to?"

"I don't know, Logan. How can I just forget about her? She got under my skin." She stepped closer to him and put her hand on his arm. "But so did you."

"Meaning?" he practically grit out.

She stepped back. "Meaning I understand how you feel."

"You just don't care," he said.

"Of course I care. But it's not that black-and-white. Clearly," she added a little too pointedly.

He glared at her. "Don't use my own situation against me, Clementine."

Her shoulder slumped. "I'm not meaning to. This all took me by surprise too. I wasn't expecting to be here right now, saying these things to you."

All the things that made Clementine stand here and say these things to him were the very reasons he'd hired her to babysit the twins last spring. Kind. Softhearted. Compassionate. But once again, his life was out of his control. He didn't like that. At all.

"Logan," she said softly. "I don't want to make things harder for you. I know you're dealing with enough as it is. But how can I just walk away from that girl, knowing she's about to be moved again and then probably again?" Tears came to her eyes and she covered her face with her hands.

He walked over to her, took her hands and just held them for a moment, then let them go. He had no answer, didn't want to say anything. He just wanted to blink himself back to some other time when everything was hunky-dory. But when? When the hell hadn't something blasted him from his everyday existence? He'd been thrown from a horse and bull a time or two or three when he was younger and almost lost his chance at a rodeo career. He'd lost his parents. He'd lost his brother. He'd been betrayed by a rival's con-woman sister in the most devious and embarrassing way. He'd discovered he wasn't his father's son. He wouldn't want to blink himself back to any of those times. Now, there was Phoebe, Parsons's ex-stepdaughter, alone in the world. Except Clementine Hurley wanted to take her in.

"Logan," she said softly. "I can only do what feels right to me. Sometimes that's all you can go by when you're conflicted about something. And this does feel right. I don't even know if CPS will let me take her in. But I want to petition to foster her."

He turned away again, looking out at the inky darkness of the front yard.

"Sleep on it," she said and left, closing the door gently behind her.

Then she came back in, rushed over to him and gripped him in a hug that caught him so off guard he hugged her back, the feel of her in his arms more welcome than he'd expected right now.

"Sleep on it," she whispered, then rushed away again.

Chapter Five

Three thirty p.m. on Monday couldn't come fast enough for Clementine. For the next two hours, she would have to stop thinking about, talking about and wondering about fostering Phoebe Pike—and how it would affect a certain cowboy. How it would change her own life. She'd been unable to think of anything else from the moment she and Logan had left Phoebe and driven home to Blue Gulch. At that point, the thought of fostering Phoebe had just been floating in her mind—*could* she? Was the universe trying to tell her something by the unexpected meeting?

She'd gone to Tuckerville with Logan—not expected.

They'd found themselves visiting a foster home—not expected.

She'd met a child in need of a home, a child with a connection to the man she loved—not expected.

During that car ride home, she kept sneaking peeks at Logan, who'd been silent, the radio not even on this time, which meant he was thinking too, about what exactly, she hadn't been sure. That Parsons's ex-stepdaughter was alone in the world? That Logan was her rodeo hero? That the man he thought he hated, the man who'd walked away from his pregnant mother without a backward glance had done at least one wonderful thing in his life: taken on the care of a child.

She knew during the hour-drive home that Logan was letting all that sit, taking it in, turning it over. So she'd stayed silent about what was flitting through her own head: the shimmer of an idea of Phoebe Pike possibly being the foster child that Clementine would be assigned.

It seemed meant to be to Clementine. But Logan's feelings couldn't be discounted. He wanted nothing to do with Clyde Turnbull Parsons and his history and legacy, and Phoebe was a part of that; she stood for who he was, not who Logan needed him to be in his mind to make sense of how the man had abandoned his mother. He needed Parsons to be a terrible person so he could close the chapter on the letter he'd received, so it would be tidy and make sense.

But Phoebe threw a big monkey wrench into that.

When Clementine had gotten home on Saturday night, she'd gone straight to her attic bedroom and flopped down on her bed, thinking, thinking, thinking. Of everything the aide had said, of everything the foster mother, Mrs. Nivens, had said, of everything Phoebe had told them.

My mother told me to always remember she loves me...

Clementine's birth mother had said those exact words to her—twice, when she was very young and she remembered how much those words meant. Even now, they meant something. Yes, Phoebe Pike had gotten inside Clementine's heart. Then at midnight, she'd texted Logan and driven over and told him what she wanted—needed—to do. Sunday came and went without a word from him, and she hadn't pressed him. She already felt she wasn't being fair to him as it was. Fair. Right. Sometimes the difference between the two was so hard to figure out—which was the one that should win out.

This morning she'd called the Texas Department of Family and Protective Services and got the number for the local office that handled Tuckerville. Just to have it, to be ready if Logan called her and gave his blessing. Then she'd realized she could at least speed up the process of getting her paperwork signed off on. Three calls and one drive to Tuckerville later, Clementine was now officially eligible to foster a child in the state of Texas.

And if Logan told her today that he absolutely did not want her to foster Phoebe, that she was butting into his business in the worst way and had no right to do this?

She let out a deep breath and closed her eyes. Right now, she had to put this all away. She had a room full of adorable children to direct, thirty-four altogether, and her full attention needed to be on breaking up the kids into groups, assigning her volunteer leaders, handing out scripts and doing a run-through of the play's first act. It was a lot for two hours, but it would be done. If Clementine focused.

At 3:31, as she stood on the stage and looked over the kids and volunteers sitting in the first few rows, she noticed the Grainger twins hadn't arrived. Maybe Logan was pulling them from the play? Would he do that?

"Sorry we're late!" called out the voice of the twins' sitter, Karen, as she ushered Henry and Harry in.

As the boys sat down at the end of the row and Karen left, Clementine breathed a sigh of relief. Logan wasn't cutting ties between them. That was good. But it also wasn't lost on her that he hadn't brought the boys in himself.

The group of youngest kids, ages two through four, started fussing in their seats, so Clementine announced groups to get the wiggle-worms up and moving and doing something fun. The volunteers and kids split up and formed circles. The leaders would be sharing with the kids what parts they had and what songs they needed to learn. For the show, the youngest group of kids were all ranchers with no speaking parts, but they would be part of the ensemble for songs. Clementine flitted from group to group, making sure everyone was doing okay.

From the corner of her eye she noticed someone come through the door. Clementine glanced over and froze. Holding a flyer and looking around the room was Lacey Woolen.

Her birth mother.

"Excuse me for a minute," Clementine said to her tween group leader, then walked over to where Lacey stood by the door. Her shoulder-length dark hair, same color and heavy straight texture as Clementine's, was in a low ponytail. She wore her usual long skirt and cowboy boots with a rust-colored suede jacket and had a silver ring on every finger, some with multiple rings.

Lacey was glancing at the flyer in her hand, more to avoid eye contact with Clementine, she thought. Why did their relationship, if that was even the right word, have to be so awkward? As Clementine approached, Lacey offered a tight smile.

"I understand you're looking for volunteers," Lacey said, her gaze going around the room where various groups were sitting in circles, some reading over song lyrics sheets, some practicing first stanzas.

Every time Clementine saw Lacey she thought about how alike they looked, the hair, the height—both tall— the pale brown eyes. Sometimes it unnerved her and made her think about her birth story, how exactly she'd come to be.

Clementine had been told by her caseworker when she turned eighteen that Lacey had shared a brief version of events; eighteen-year-old Lacey had been deeply in love with a substance-abusing young man her age, but he'd been long gone before Lacey had even discovered she was pregnant. Then five years after Clementine was born, Lacey had learned he had died. Clementine looked at Lacey now and wished the two of them could just sit and talk about all this—Lacey's past, how Lacey had felt about her baby's father, all that. But Clementine had to accept it was never going to happen.

Clementine did have to admit though that seeing Lacey walking into the room, flyer in her hand soliciting volunteers to help with the children's Christmas show, was a surprise.

"I'd like to help with singing," Lacey added. "I do love to sing."

I remember, Clementine thought, feeling a pinch in her chest. She didn't have many memories of living with Lacey, but she did remember her singing her to sleep several times. And she also remembered the angelic voice, almost as if it was magical that a real person, her mother at that, could have such a voice.

"I'm very glad you've come," Clementine said, trying to inject nonchalance into her voice. In the past, too much emotion, whether enthusiasm or need or anger, would send the woman running away. "Do you have a particular age group you'd like to work with?" Clementine asked. "I could use the most help with the five-to-eights since they're old enough to learn the songs but have the toughest time memorizing."

"That's fine," Lacey said.

Clementine led Lacey over to the group of kids and introduced her to the children and the two other volunteers, then hurried away in the pretext of checking in with the teenagers, who seemed to be having a squabble. By the time she reached that group, the volunteers had defused the tension between two girls and all was well.

Clementine glanced over at Lacey. She was nodding in encouragement at two seven-year-old boys as they sang the first stanza of "Jingle Bells." *Why are you here?* she wondered. *What do you want? Why do you keep on the fringes? What the heck is it going to take to make you bust through and want to know who I am? To let me know who you are? Why are you so frustrating?*

When Clementine would pose these questions to her

grandmother over the years as she'd notice Lacey peering in the restaurant windows, coming in for lunch yet making sure to sit at another waitress's table, walking past the Victorian and just staring up at the windows, her gram would say that her birth mother clearly wanted to feel connected to Clementine at a level she could handle and that you had to let people have their levels.

But that's not fair, Clementine would say back. *Why does she get to decide the level? Why don't I? I'm the one with the questions.*

And her grandmother would just hold her close and say her birth mother might not ever be ready to answer those questions; she might never get any closer than another waitress's table. *You may not know everything you want to know about Lacey, but you do know who you are, Clementine Hurley. And that someone is pretty special.*

Then Clementine would cry at how sweet her grandmother was and for how frustrated she was, but at least she'd feel better.

But that's not fair...why does she get to decide the level? Why don't I?

Clementine bit her lip, realizing that Logan had said as much about the two of them on Saturday night. Why did Clementine get to decide something that had such huge emotional repercussions for him?

At the sound of laughter, Clementine glanced over at the youngest group, Henry Grainger doubled over in glee, his brother looking so angry she was afraid he'd lash out. She hurried over.

"What's going on here, guys?" she asked, looking from twin to twin.

"Henry told me I keep saying the wrong word, but I didn't!" Henry shouted.

"It's jingle all the way, not jingle on the hay," Harry said, trying not to laugh again.

"It is jingle all the way," Clementine said. "But I'll bet you have hay on your mind because you were decorating the horses' Christmas tree in the barn. Am I right, Henry?"

Henry nodded. "Uncle Logan said we can put presents under the tree for them. I'm drawing Lulu and Winnie a picture."

"Oh me too," Harry said. "Let's draw a giant one from both of us."

And just like that, the squabble was over. Clementine put out a few more of these fires with the help of her volunteers over the next two hours, but headway with a few different songs was made. Clementine had avoided contact with Lacey during the rehearsal, pretty sure her birth mother wanted it that way. She wanted Lacey to come back. She glanced over at the woman, smiling at a little boy as he barely got through the first stanza of "Jingle Bells." As Lacey began to sing, the area around her quieted as her beautiful voice floated through the room. When Lacey finished and the little boy began to try the stanza again, Clementine forced her attention away. Why *were* people so complicated?

"There are my guys," came a familiar voice.

Clementine whirled around to see Logan walking

up to the twins. He knelt down and held up a palm for two high fives.

He looked so damned gorgeous. He wore a navy shirt that made his blue eyes even more intense and a dark brown leather jacket over jeans.

"Can Clementine come over for dinner?" Harry asked.

"Say yes, Uncle Logan," Henry pleaded.

Logan stiffened. But he looked at her and said, "The restaurant is closed on Mondays so you don't have to work, right?"

This was a surprise.

"Are you inviting me over for dinner?" she asked.

"The boys did. And I think we should talk," he added in a lower voice. He turned to the twins. "Guys, why don't you go say goodbye and thank you to your counselors?" They went sprinting over to Jackie and Heather, who were straightening chairs and putting song sheets back in bins for the next rehearsal.

Hope blossomed. Would he invite her to dinner to tell her she didn't have his blessing? No way. He'd just blurt it out on the sidewalk so he could escape rather than have her in his house where she could state her case, explain herself and ask him to rethink.

"If you're going to…" He cleared his throat. "I think we should discuss how that's going to go. You mentioned Phoebe working at my ranch, for example. I don't know about that."

The hope blossomed brighter. Perhaps she did have his blessing. He was trying to set ground rules. "Well,

I haven't yet petitioned to foster Phoebe. I didn't want to do that until I heard from you."

She needed his blessing. Truth be told, she was scared spitless about taking in Phoebe. She *wanted* to take in Phoebe. Very, very much so. But she'd never been responsible for anyone before, let alone a child, a girl who'd been through her share of hurts and losses and disappointments, a girl who'd been shunted around. Clementine had her family's support and her own experience to guide her, but given the twisty way she'd come into Clementine's orbit, she did want Logan Grainger's blessing.

He looked away, glancing out the window, then at the many parents coming to collect their kids from rehearsal.

"Are you okay with it?" she whispered.

He looked at her, his expression unreadable. "I don't know that I'm okay with it. I just understand why you want to—and should."

She gasped. "Logan. Thank you. Really, thank you. That means a lot to me."

He stepped closer. "The thought of her at that home with a foster mother who doesn't seem to like her at all…I can't say it didn't bother me. 'She wants to be a bronc rider…rodeo clown is where she's headed.' I didn't like that. Not one bit."

Clementine nodded. "I didn't either."

He leaned his head back. "I don't know anything, Clementine. I guess the only thing I do know is that what you said the other day makes sense."

"What was that?" she asked.

"That sometimes all you can go by is what you feel is right. Heck, I don't feel it's right just leaving her there, but I'm not prepared to do anything about it. So I'm glad you will."

God, she wanted to fling herself into his arms and hug him tight and never let him go.

Logan kissed each nephew on the forehead and drew up their rodeo-imprinted comforters to their chests, then quietly left their bedroom and headed back downstairs. After dinner, an impromptu game of tag in the yard and some decorating of the house Christmas tree, Clementine had brought the boys upstairs to read them a bedtime story. Logan had peeked in toward the end, touched at how she truly seemed to adore his nephews, answering their many *But why?* questions about the stories, her voice laced with affection. She'd slipped past him so he could say his good-nights even though they were snoring away, and the barest scent of perfume had caught him and caused a reaction he hadn't expected.

She'd caused a reaction. He was so damned attracted to her. Sometimes he was glad for it; lately, he'd be talking to her about something uncomfortable that made him want to claw his chest, like the whole thing with Parsons, with Phoebe, and he'd suddenly be overtaken by how sexy Clementine was, all that long silky dark hair and her lush curves. Everything would go out of his head but Clementine. She was straightforward and for the most part serious, not a flirtatious bone to be found, and she drew him unlike any woman ever had. He had no idea how she managed to clear his mind of everything but her when she was a constant reminder of all the turmoil in his life.

He came down the stairs and found her standing in front of the big window overlooking the side pasture. Again he was struck by how her jeans and soft pink sweater hugged her tall, slender body. She'd taken off her cowboy boots and wore yellow socks. He tried to focus on the socks, to get his mind off how pretty she was, how much he wanted her. It was working, actually.

"They're fast asleep," he said.

She turned around and he forgot the socks. "I made two mugs of tea," she said, pointing at the coffee table. He glanced at the tray with the mugs and sugar bowl and creamer.

"Thanks. Does a splash or two or five of whiskey go in tea?" he asked.

She offered a small smile and walked over to the sofa and sat down, wrapping her hand around the yellow mug. "It's big stuff, I know. For you, for me. But Logan, it really does feel absolutely right to me to foster Phoebe."

He picked up the other mug and added a teaspoon of sugar and a splash of cream, wishing it really was the whiskey. "Well, given your history, I can understand that. And clearly, since you had this all set in motion for months now—I mean, to become a foster mother—I can see how A led to B."

She was quiet for a moment, wrapping her hand around her mug of tea, the steam rising. "My birth mother came to volunteer today. She's helping with singing."

"You okay?"

She nodded. "Well, okay enough. She makes me feel so…unsteady, I guess."

"I know what that's like," he said.

"You sure do." She reached over and squeezed his hand and he wanted to pull her to him and hold her. They could both use a good hug. But then he remembered why she was here, why he'd invited her. To talk through how things would work when—if—Phoebe came to live with her.

"Speaking of birth mothers," he said. "How does this work with Phoebe's? You foster her but she can't be adopted, like you were?"

"Well, it's possible that her mother's parental rights could be involuntarily terminated due to prolonged abandonment. But that would be something for the caseworkers and a family court judge and I, if I'm her foster mother, to discuss in the future."

"The hospice aide was right," Logan said. "Phoebe has been dealt a rough hand."

Clementine nodded. "So you can understand why I was so moved by her story. I was prepared to take in whatever child was matched with me," she said, sipping her tea. "But meeting Phoebe, listening to her, knowing some of her story, her connection to you, that she was going to be moved again—I found myself unable to stop thinking about her."

He'd been thinking about Phoebe too. The way her eyes had lit up at the sight of him. That she had Parsons's scrapbook with rodeo ticket stubs and flyers and newspaper articles. The story the hospice aide had told, all that Phoebe had said, that the foster mother had said. Everything had been flying around in his head, smashing into one another, making his chest feeling heavy.

Clementine sipped her tea. "And suddenly the faceless, nameless child I'd been mentally preparing myself for became very real."

He nodded and leaned his head back, then sat up straighter, resting his hands on his thighs. "*Very real* might just be the key words here, Clementine. That girl is a very real reminder to me that Parsons was real, that he existed, even though he's gone. He was taking care of her even though she was the kid of the wife who'd left him. And knowing he was dying, he made arrangements for her, thinking she'd be okay. Part of me hates that I can't write him off as a total bastard."

Clementine nodded. "I know."

"But I want to, Clem. And I don't want to know anything about him. I just want to forget him and the letter—all of it. I want to go on believing that Haywood Grainger was my father. And with you bringing Phoebe to Blue Gulch, Parsons becomes impossible not to think about."

"Maybe that's not such a bad thing, though," she said. "For you to be forced to deal with the truth, how you feel about it."

He shoved the mug back on the table and stood up. "I know how I feel about it. I hate it."

She stood up too and took his hands. "You don't have to have any involvement. Or you could take slow steps. Or no steps."

She was watching him, gauging. She expected him to take some steps. And that wasn't fair.

He pulled away from her and shoved his hands in his pockets. "I told you—I don't know about this, Clem. I don't know if I want anything to do with her at all. And you can't make me feel bad about that. That's not fair."

She took a breath. "You're right. I know you're right. And I know that I am overstepping here, Logan. I want you to be comfortable with this. As much as you can be, anyway."

"What the hell happened to my life?" he asked, dropping down on the sofa. "One minute, I'm eight seconds on a bull, walking away with a wad of prize money, and the next, I'm pulling photographs out of a PO box, discovering my entire damned life was a lie."

"Not a lie, Logan. Your father was your father. He raised you. He was there. He loved you, he was responsible for you. He was your father."

He leaned over and drew her to him, those words meaning so much to him that he lost control of himself and went by pure need. And that need was to have her in his arms. His hands slid to either side of her face and he looked at her, beautiful Clementine with her big pale brown eyes, and there was so much in those eyes that he closed his and kissed her hard and deep and long, hoping she'd relax against him instead of the ramrod straightness and then she did. In that moment, everything inside him let go. All he saw, all he thought about was Clementine.

"I've missed this," he said. "Even though we had

just one kiss, I'd thought about kissing you constantly. I could barely think straight."

She smiled and slipped her arms around his neck. "Me too."

"Just for tonight, let's just forget everything but us and this," he said. He kissed her again and she melted into him, deepening the kiss, her lush breasts against his chest, the scent of her spicy perfume teasing him, tantalizing him. He slid a hand under her soft yellow sweater, up past her stomach to the bottom edge of her lacy bra. He had to know what color it was.

Yes, yes, yes, he thought, every single thing they'd been talking about going out of his head. Bras. Breasts. Clementine kissing him. That's all he wanted—all other thoughts obliterated. His other hand slid under the sweater and he ran both over the wisp of bra, her full breasts against his hands. He pressed her against the sofa until he was half lying on top of her, every part of him straining and buckling. He needed her naked. Now.

He pulled up the sweater and drank in the sight of her. The bra was black.

"Logan," she whispered. Her hands were on his face, drawing his head upward. "Logan, I don't know if this is a good idea."

"This is a good idea," he said, moving to the other breast, trying to lose himself again in the sensations and scent and feel of her.

"And tomorrow morning? In the bright light of day? When you've had coffee and everything we've talked about is still hovering between us? Will it be a good idea then? When we can add had sex to an already complicated situation?"

Oh hell. He closed his eyes and jerked himself upward and away from her, hating that she was right.

She sat up, straightening the black bra and pulling down her sweater in one quick move, her cheeks reddened. "The last time you kissed me you didn't speak to me for three months."

He dropped his head in his hands. "I'm sorry I hurt you. I'm sorry I was a jerk. I couldn't handle my life then and I'm not doing a great job now."

"You are handling it, though," she said, her voice softening. "You went to that PO box. You went to Tuckerville again. To the hospice. You spoke to the aide. You met Phoebe. You gave me your blessing to foster her. You *are* handling it. You're not sticking your head in the sand."

He ran a hand through his thick, dark hair. "I want to."

She smiled. "I know. And I have a feeling that this, I mean, what just happened between us, was part of that. But it'll just add another level of complication for both of us, Logan. Sex means something to me. It's not about forgetting my life or having an orgasm. Sex means… love to me, Logan."

He turned away, unable, no, unwilling, to continue this conversation. He wanted her desperately but he didn't want to think beyond right now. He had enough on his plate, on his mind.

She sat up straight. "If I do get to foster Phoebe, I think it would be very good for the two of you to be in each other's lives. She doesn't know you're Parsons's biological child. She only knows you as her bull-riding hero. It's up to you to tell her or not about your connection to her stepfather. But I do think the two of you could do each other a world of good."

Too much, too fast. His temple was beginning to throb.

"I'm raising two boys alone, Clementine," he practically grit out. "I have a ranch to run. I don't have time or resources to be her hero just because of some light-weight connection between us."

"Logan, I thought we were going to talk about ground rules for how things would work if I foster Phoebe. But I think we've gone as far as we can on the subject tonight."

"I think we've said all there is to say on the subject, period."

She stood up and walked to the door and grabbed her jacket from the coatrack. "I don't think we have," she said, her voice softer. "In the morning I'm going to call Phoebe's caseworker and let her know I'm a foster parent who'd like to take in Phoebe. I'm going to explain how we're connected, if that's all right with you. I do think we should be honest about how I came to meet Phoebe."

He walked as far as the archway that separated the foyer from the living room. "Okay."

She looked at him, then opened the door and walked out, taking a piece of himself with her.

Chapter Six

Clementine was working on her Creole sauce on Thursday morning when the call came from Phoebe's caseworker. She was approved to foster Phoebe! Apparently, after Clementine had called the caseworker two days ago, there had been a rush of calls and meetings to discuss Phoebe's situation and all was now in order for Phoebe to come live with Clementine. Clementine would need to drive out to Tuckerville tomorrow to sign some paperwork and be briefed on specifics relating to Phoebe, and then on Saturday, Phoebe would arrive at the apricot Victorian to live.

Clementine clicked off her cell phone and squeezed her eyes shut as a feeling of happiness tingled up her nerve endings. This was happening.

"Clem?" her sister Annabel said, eyeing Clementine

from her grill station. She flipped over chicken breasts, slathering the meat with marinade. "Did you just get very good news or very bad news? I can't tell."

"I want to laugh and cry at the same time—out of happiness and a little fear," Clementine said. "That was Phoebe's caseworker. I've been approved to be her foster mother."

Annabel and Georgia rushed over to hug Clementine, well, as much as their very pregnant bellies would allow.

Their grandmother came into the kitchen and tied on her apron. "What are we celebrating? Big reservation for lunch? Ranchers Association coming in?"

"Actually, they are," Clementine said. "I took that call myself a half hour ago. "But we're celebrating that I'm going to be a foster mother starting Saturday morning at nine!"

Clementine had told her grandmother and sisters about meeting Phoebe and her relation to Logan; all four women had been rooting for the placement to happen.

Essie Hurley gasped and clapped her hands. "Oh, Clementine. I'm so glad. You're meant to do this. And you're going to be great at it." She hugged Clementine and gave her a big kiss on the cheek.

"Today's Thursday—that gives you only two days to get her bedroom ready!" Annabel said. "What is she like? Girly girl? Tomboy? Somewhere in between?"

Her bedroom! Clementine hadn't even thought about that. Of course she'd need to decorate a bedroom for a nine-year-old girl. Right now, the three second-floor bedrooms were guest-friendly, but nothing that would make a nine-year-old girl feel particularly at home—

or happy. "Well, from what I've seen and the bit I've heard from the caseworker, she's definitely a tomboy. She loves the rodeo. Logan is her rodeo hero. She used to go to all his events."

"Cowgirl chic," Georgia said. "I can see it now."

Clementine laughed. "I think plain Western is more her style. She's also a Texas Rangers fan."

"Let's go shopping tomorrow morning at Home Style," Annabel said. "After I put Lucy on the school bus. I'll pick you all up."

"I love the idea of each of us choosing a little something for her room," Gram said. "To let her know she's part of our family now."

"You're the best, Gram," she said. "You all are. I don't know what I'd do without you three."

Georgia smiled. "That goes ditto for me."

"And me," Annabel said.

Clementine had goose bumps. This was exactly what Clementine wanted for Phoebe. Love and family and support. And goose bumps—in a good way.

On Thursday afternoon, Logan was grooming his favorite horse, a beautiful brown-and-white mare named Sundappled, when he saw Clementine's little navy car coming up the long gravel driveway to the ranch. She hadn't called. Which told Logan she must have news she felt was worthy of a personal delivery.

He braced himself. He'd been bracing himself ever since she'd come over the other night and told him she wanted to foster Phoebe. He'd avoided her all week, having Karen drop off the boys at Monday's and

Wednesday's Christmas show rehearsal. He'd been busy. A section of fence had been damaged by a fallen tree during Sunday's rainstorm, and his ranch hand had called in sick on Wednesday. Logan had been glad for all the extra work; it had been easy to stay away from town, from the town hall, from Hurley's Homestyle Kitchen and from thinking too much about Clementine's plans to foster Phoebe.

But he hadn't been able to stop thinking about how she'd felt in his arms. How much he wanted her. The past few nights, while he lay in bed he thought of little else but kissing Clementine, the way she'd kissed him back, that lacy bra.

He put down the grooming brush and adjusted his Stetson, then walked over to where she'd parked.

She got out of the car and pushed her sunglasses up on top of her head. "Sorry for just turning up like this. But I wanted to talk to you face-to-face."

He waited.

"A little while ago I heard from Phoebe's caseworker. I'm approved to foster her. She's going to arrive Saturday at nine."

There it was. Official and done. He let it sit for a second. He wasn't jumping out of his skin the way he'd been for so long after getting Parsons's letter. Phoebe would be coming to live with Clementine, that was a fact, and he would deal with it. "Well, I'm happy for both of you, Clementine. I know this has been a dream of yours for a long time. And any kid would be lucky to have you as a foster mother."

He hadn't even meant to say that; the words had

just tumbled out of his mouth, straight from the deepest part of him.

She rushed over and hugged him. "Thank you, Logan. Sometimes you say exactly the right thing just when I need to hear it most."

He hugged her back, then stepped away a bit, giving himself some distance from all the emotion on her face—happiness, fear, concern, excitement. "I'm glad to hear that. I usually say the wrong thing at the right time."

She smiled. "I'm going to be a foster mother," she said with wonder in her voice. "I'm going to be able to give back what was given to me by my parents."

"I know you will," he said, picturing Phoebe in her Texas Rangers cap at the second-floor window of the home she lived in now.

For the past few days he'd been trying to imagine how things would go if Phoebe came to live with Clementine. If he'd pay a visit or not. He still wasn't sure.

You gave her your card with your cell phone number, he reminded himself. *She could easily just call you and ask you questions about the rodeo. You'll have to talk to her.*

Why had he done that? The girl wanted his autograph and he'd scrawled it on the back of his card—pointedly. He'd felt for her during their lunch as she'd talked about her situation, what she'd been through. And when Mrs. Nivens had made that crack about how a career as a rodeo clown was more up her alley than bronc rider, he'd been glad he'd given Phoebe his number. She hadn't used it. At first he was afraid she'd call constantly, pestering him with "remember this, remember that" about his events and championships. But she hadn't.

"Well, I'd better get back and help with the dinner prep and dining room set up," she said, squinting up at him in the bright sunshine.

"I'm glad it all worked out," he said. "I mean that. I might not be all that comfortable with it, but like I said, I'm glad for the two of you."

"I know you are," she said. He had the feeling she wanted to say something else, but she just reached out a hand to his arm and then turned and got back in her car. He watched her car drive away until it was out of sight.

Saturday morning, Phoebe Pike arrived at the Victorian with two suitcases. Phoebe's shoulder-length sandy-brown hair was in a low ponytail under a Texas Rangers baseball cap. She wore a red T-shirt advertising a Stocktown rodeo, blue jeans and bright orange sneakers. She had a yellow backpack hanging off one shoulder.

Ellen Moncrief, her caseworker, smiled at Clementine and her grandmother who waited on the porch. The girl stood staring up at the house, taking in the sign reading Hurley's Homestyle Kitchen, the front garden, the people walking around Blue Gulch Street and going in and out of shops.

"I'm so happy you're here," Clementine said, rushing down the porch steps to meet them.

"I still can't believe it," Phoebe said, putting down her suitcases. "Why would you want to take me in? My own aunt doesn't want me."

Clementine's heart squeezed. "Well, like Ellen told

you, for the past several months I've been working on becoming a foster mother. And when I met you and heard your story, I thought we might be a good match for each other."

Part of Clementine wanted to tell Phoebe the entire story so that everything was in the open, but Ellen thought that the right time would reveal itself.

"I'll be living in a restaurant?" Phoebe asked, glancing up at the sign, her hazel eyes full of wonder.

Essie Hurley laughed and came down to meet Phoebe. "Well, we do live in this Victorian, which also houses Hurley's Homestyle Kitchen. But there are three bedrooms on the second floor and Clementine's on the third floor." Essie extended her hand toward Phoebe. "I'm Essie Hurley, Clementine's grandmother. I'm so happy you've come to live with us. I hope you like cheeseburgers because that's one of our specials for lunch today."

"I love cheeseburgers," Phoebe said.

"Me too," Clementine added. "Why don't we go show you the house and your room?"

Ellen said her goodbyes to Phoebe, reminding her of a few details and how to get in touch.

Clementine picked up the suitcases and let her gram lead the way. So far, so good. Phoebe had to be nervous. This morning, when Ellen had called to confirm the drop-off time, she'd let Clementine know to expect attitude and tears and push back and to not take anything personally or respond to drama—only to what was behind the attitude: fear. *Soothe the fears*, Ellen had said.

Clementine remembered walking into Clinton and

Charlaine Hurley's pretty white house across town for the first time when she was eight, staring up at it just the way Phoebe had the Victorian, overcome with fear and hope in equal measure.

Now, Clementine stepped into the house, through the round parlor that served as a waiting area for the restaurant and overlooked the large archway to the dining room off to the left. Now, at just after nine, the restaurant wasn't open, but the kitchen was busy in preparation for lunch.

"I smell something amazing," Phoebe said, sniffing the air.

"That's lunch prep," Clementine explained. "The restaurant opens at eleven, so the kitchen staff is hard at work."

"Speaking of kitchen staff, I'd better get back to it," Gram said. "Phoebe, again, I'm so happy you're here. And remember, this is your home too now. You can call me Gram, Gram Hurley or Essie—whichever you prefer."

A shy smile lit Phoebe's face, but she didn't say anything.

Essie went into the kitchen, Phoebe watching her.

"I've never had a grandmother," Phoebe said.

"Gram is a great one. When my parents first brought me to live with them when I was eight, she immediately made me feel like part of the family. I never forgot that."

Phoebe hitched her yellow backpack higher on her shoulder. "Ellen told me you were in foster care when you were a kid. I guess you know what it's like then."

"Sure do. Which is one of the reasons I want you to

feel at home here. I know you just got here and it may take a few days for you to settle in, but this is home."

Phoebe glanced up at her, then at the pictures lining the walls and then out the windows.

Clementine waited a beat in case Phoebe wanted to keep on this track. She'd learned in her classes about fostering children that if they wanted to talk about being in foster care or about their families or if they had questions, even if they were tough ones, it was better to let them talk and to answer as honestly as possible in a way that soothed. Clementine sure hoped she didn't make any mistakes. Phoebe seemed very forthright, but she was young.

"Can I see my room?" Phoebe asked.

Clementine breathed a sigh of relief. This was an easy part. She and her sisters had spent two hours at Home Style yesterday morning buying everything from cute table lamps with cacti as bases and funky yellow-and-white shades, a dusty orange soft comforter with lassos embroidered all over it and matching shams, an orange shag rug in the shape of a bull, which Annabel had squealed over, and a bunch of desk-related items—from school supplies to a corkboard. They'd decided on the medium-sized bedroom with the view of Blue Gulch Street, since it had a window seat where Phoebe could sit and read or just watch people as they walked up and down the shopping area. Her sisters had really seemed to enjoy helping decorate the room. All three Hurley women had had experience with loss and moving into a new home, albeit with their grandmother, and they all wanted to help make Phoebe's room a sweet sanctuary.

Clementine led the way upstairs and opened the door. Phoebe stepped in.

"This is mine?" she said, eyes wide, mouth open as she glanced around.

Clementine nodded. "My sisters and I set it up. I hope you like it."

"I love the lasso blanket and pillows," Phoebe said. "And the lamps. And the rug. But it's just missing one thing."

Clementine tilted her head. "What's that?"

"Is it okay if I put a poster up on the wall?"

"Of course."

Phoebe headed in and set her backpack on the desk, pulling out a rolled-up poster. "Will you help me put it up? I'd like it to go right beside the corkboard."

"Sure," Clementine said.

As Phoebe unrolled it, Clementine could see the handsome face of Logan Grainger, then his shoulders and torso and the rest of him. He was upright on a bucking bull, one hand up in the air, the other on the bull rope. Clementine stared at the poster, at the man she'd been unable to stop thinking about for months.

Phoebe held up the poster, positioning it where she wanted beside the corkboard. "I still can't believe I had lunch with Logan Grainger. Three-time champion. And he would have won the last time but for some reason he didn't show up."

"Maybe that was when he went home to care for his nephews."

"Nah, it was a month before that. I heard about that, when his brother and his wife died and he quit rodeo to take care of his little nephews. Clyde, my stepfather, told me all about it. He said that made Logan the biggest champ ever."

Clementine's heart squeezed. "That was a nice thing to say. And I agree."

As Clementine helped Phoebe tape up the poster of Logan, she took in the man in question. She wondered why he hadn't shown up for the championship. Maybe it had something to do with that talk of the Handcuff Cowboy Phoebe had brought up at lunch and Logan had quickly shut down.

"I can't believe Logan Grainger lives right here in Blue Gulch too. I hope I can see him around."

"I'm sure you will," Clementine said, wondering how that would work out.

They spent the next half hour putting away Phoebe's things, Clementine smiling at the tomboy's clothes. Phoebe was very much into jeans and T-shirts and baseball caps. She did own one dress that had seen better days. During the shopping trip, Clementine's sister Georgia had kept wanting to girly up the room, but Clementine had reminded her Phoebe seemed very much a tomboy, which Ellen had confirmed, and so Clementine had nixed pink and purple and boas. A collection of baseball hats now hung on the row of pegs by the door along with a jean jacket.

Phoebe sat down at the desk and Clementine thought she might leave for a little while to give the girl some privacy, but Phoebe said, "And now, for the final touches." She pulled out two framed photographs from the backpack. "This is my mother. Isn't she pretty?"

Clementine stepped over and took the photograph in a silver frame. The woman was very pretty. She had Phoebe's big hazel eyes, but her hair was platinum blond. She had her arms around a younger Phoebe, who must have been about seven years old in the photo.

"That's the last time I saw my mom," Phoebe said. "Before she left us to move to Las Vegas. I think she'll probably come get me for Christmas. Clyde always told me not to get my hopes up about my mother coming back and I know it's not like she paid much attention to me before she left, but maybe she had to get some stuff worked out of her system. Clyde used to say that too."

Clementine's heart pinged. Ellen had warned her that Phoebe had high hopes about her mother, that she would come for Christmas and finally take her back. Ellen had had the very hard conversation with Phoebe three months ago that her mother might not ever come back, that it had been two years since she left. Apparently, the woman had been tracked to Amsterdam when Phoebe's aunt had tried to locate her after Clyde had died, but Phoebe's mother had changed her name and was impossible to find and seemingly wanted to stay that way.

Phoebe is in an understandable state of denial about it, Ellen had said. *She knows the truth, but can't handle the truth, and this is how she's dealing with it. As Christmas approaches, it'll be especially hard as she waits for her mother to show up and she doesn't.*

Oh, Phoebe, Clementine thought, watching the girl set the picture just so on her desk, moving it this way and that until she liked the angle.

Then she picked up the second photograph. It was Clyde Parsons, no doubt. Clementine knew that instantly from having seen the photo Logan had shown her from twenty-eight years ago. Here he was in his late forties, but it was clearly him. He looked so much like Logan it was a wonder Phoebe had never noticed the resemblance.

"This is Clyde, my stepfather," Phoebe said. "I can't believe he's gone. It's been three months but it feels like longer." She was looking at the picture, a wistful expression on her face. "Isn't it funny that he wasn't even related to me but took care of me two whole years since my mother left?"

The more Clementine heard about Clyde, the more she liked the man he'd become. "One thing I've learned from my own history is that family isn't just about who gave birth to you or whose DNA you have."

Phoebe didn't say anything. She set up the photograph of Clyde Parsons on the other side of the desk, adjusting it just so as she'd done with the one of her mother.

Maybe it was time for a change of subject. "Ready for an amazing cheeseburger?" Clementine asked. "My sister Annabel and our apprentice cook, Dylan, are on the grill today. Best burgers ever. Except for my grandmother's. No one cooks like my gram."

"I'm *starving*," Phoebe said.

One minute, one morning, one day at a time, the caseworker had said. Phoebe would settle in, Clementine would begin feeling like a foster mother, and they'd find a routine and a comfort. Right now, Clementine had to admit her nerves were taut, more so than she'd expected. She didn't want to say the wrong thing.

She took one more look at the Logan Grainger poster up on the wall of Phoebe's room.

"I'm gonna be just like him one day," Phoebe said, raising her hand in the air as if on a bull. "Of course, I've never been on a bull, but Clyde took me for bareback riding lessons a few times and said that's a start."

"Well if you'd like to ride horses there are plenty of ranches around here," Clementine said as they headed down the stairs to the dining room. "In fact, my sister Annabel lives on a ranch. They have lots of horses and ponies."

Phoebe's eyes widened. "Could I go there sometime?"

"I'm sure. Let's go have a tour of the kitchen and you can meet Annabel and everyone. Then we'll eat."

Phoebe's face brightened. "Hey, now that I live in the same town as Logan Grainger, do you think I could go over to his ranch sometime? He could give me pointers on how to get into the rodeo when I'm older. I know he gave me his card with his phone number, but I'd feel funny just calling him up. It would be like calling the president, you know?" She titled her head. "Maybe you could ask him for me? Please? Please with a million pleases on top?"

Clementine laughed, but her stomach was churning. "I'll see what I can do," she said and led the way into the kitchen. Luckily, for the moment the conversation came to a halt since the Hurley's Homestyle Kitchen staff made a big welcoming fuss over Phoebe. Annabel indeed invited her over to the ranch this week, Georgia offered baking lessons once she heard Phoebe liked baking, and Dylan, the eighteen-year-old cook, let Phoebe flip the burger he was making for her, then add two kinds of cheese.

Clementine hung back, her worries dissipating as her heart filled with gratitude.

Now there was just the matter of Phoebe's big hope to see her hero.

Logan had planned on having the twins' sitter drop them off at the Christmas show rehearsal on Monday, but he realized doing so himself would allow him a quick hello to Phoebe and he could cross that off the list of things that were keeping him awake at night. Clementine had texted him two days ago to let him know that Phoebe had arrived on Saturday morning and was settling in.

He'd show up, welcome her to Blue Gulch, then hightail it out of there. In an indirect way, Clementine had done him a favor by fostering Phoebe. Since he didn't want Phoebe to be a part of his life, he'd have to avoid Clementine. And avoiding Clementine was what he'd been successful at doing for the past three months—until he'd gone and opened up to her, telling her about the letter, asking her to come with him to Tuckerville. Now that Phoebe was living with her, the girl a walking, talking reminder that Parsons had been a real person who'd done at least one good thing in his life, Logan was even more determined to forget Parsons entirely, forget the whole sorry thing.

It bothered him, this good side of Parsons. He hadn't

done some one-shot good deed; raising Phoebe for two years had been ongoing. The minute Parsons knew his ex-wife wasn't coming back, he didn't try to send Phoebe away. He'd taken care of her—for two years until the day he died.

An inconsistency that Logan didn't want to deal with. He needed Parsons to be a terrible jerk so he could tuck him away and not think about it and go on with the notion that his father was Haywood Grainger, period.

A quick hello, he assured himself as he pulled into the parking lot of the town hall, admiring the nine-foot spruce on the town green that had been decorated with what must be hundreds of strands of multicolored lights. As he and the twins headed up the steps to the building, he nodded and made small talk with other parents who were dropping off their kids. On the way to the community room, sounds of talking and laughter greeted him from every direction. Groups of singing kids and volunteers were scattered all over the room.

"I see our counselor!" Harry said. "Come on, Henry!"

"Bye, Uncle Logan!" Henry said and the two boys were careening across the room by the stage.

Logan glanced around for Clementine; he just wanted one glimpse of her, but didn't see her. He looked back in the direction the twins had gone in, and he didn't see or hear them either. He thought that a good thing, since Henry and Harry were often the loudest, wildest kids in any room and very easy to spot. For once, in this joyful cacophony, the Grainger boys blended.

He strained his neck to try to make them out, just to get a visual on them, and there they were, sitting in a circle group with their counselor, playing a patty-cake game to a song, a Christmas carol his mother used to sing.

"Logan!" an excited voice called out.

Logan looked up to see Phoebe running over to him. He stiffened for a second, then made himself relax. *She's just a kid, Grainger*, he reminded himself. *And innocent in everything going on in your life. It's not her fault that her ex-stepfather turned to be the biological father you never knew you had, well, other than the man who raised you. It's not her fault.*

"We're living in the same town!" Phoebe said. "Isn't that amazing? Maybe I could come see your ranch sometime. Do you keep bulls for practice?"

"I do have bulls," he said, "but for breeding and one as a pet. My rodeo days are over."

Her face fell. "Forever?"

He nodded. "'Fraid so. I've got two little boys to take care of. I can't go around risking my life the way I used to."

She seemed to think about that for a moment. "Clyde was right about you. He said he didn't know you but could tell you were a really good person just by looking at you. And then when you quit the rodeo to raise your nephews, he knew it for sure."

Logan felt himself bristle. "Well, I'm not sure you could tell much just by looking at someone." He'd thought about the fact that Parsons had come to his events at local rodeos. For days it had bothered him that there was someone out there in the world who knew something about him that he didn't know, something so fundamental, sitting right there in the stands and watching. The thought was creepy. Then just sad. Then made him angry.

Then he'd try to shut down his thoughts since they were all over the place.

Since Clementine's text about Phoebe's arrival: a zillion times worse.

He heard a bell ring and glanced up; Clementine stood on the stage and announced it was time to break into groups. He couldn't take his eyes off her. She wore a long, fuzzy red sweater, sexy black yoga pants, tall black riding boots and a Santa hat on her head that read Staff: Clementine across it in glittery neon yellow.

"I gotta go, but can I ask you something?" Phoebe said. "Clyde once told me you rescued a bull that was getting old and sick or something. One of the only ones you couldn't win on. Is that true?"

Crazy Joe. He smiled thinking about that sweet old guy who liked roaming the far pasture, no one climbing on his back. He'd heard the bull was going to be put down unless someone could take him and care for him, and Logan had gone out to Stocktown and brought him home. "He was one of my favorites," Logan said. "I think only three riders ever lasted eight seconds on Crazy Joe. I wasn't one of them."

How had Parsons heard he'd bought Crazy Joe? He shrugged away the question when he remembered he'd been interviewed about it for the Rodeo Times page in the *Tuckerville Gazette.*

"Could I meet him sometime?" she asked, her hazel eyes hopeful.

But that would entail you coming out to the ranch. Possibly getting chummy with Henry and Harry, who'd already know you from rehearsal. You'd be on my land. And you might start talking about Clyde, telling me what I don't want to know. Like how much he seemed to keep tabs on me.

"Phoebe, we need you in group," a voice called out.

Logan glanced over. A woman was standing up and smiling and waving Phoebe over.

"Time to practice my lines," Phoebe said. "I'm playing Sarah, the shepherd girl. I have nine lines. I've never been in a show before." She glanced at Logan and he realized she was hoping for an answer to her question about meeting Crazy Joe. The more she just bit her lip and hesitated instead of flat-out asking again, the more he couldn't ignore the question.

Heck. "I can talk to Clementine about a good day for you to meet Crazy Joe," he said.

Her entire face lit up. "Awesome! Thanks!" She rushed over to the group, the volunteer putting an arm around her and welcoming her.

"Who on earth is Crazy Joe?"

Logan turned around. Clementine stood there, carrying scripts and a clipboard. Her expression told him she was pleased he'd been talking to Phoebe.

"A bull from my rodeo days. One I couldn't best. He developed an illness, so I took him home and nursed him back to health. Phoebe had heard about him and asked if she could come see him sometime."

He could see relief in her face. That since he'd brought it up, maybe his answer would be yes.

"Would tomorrow after school work?" she asked. "No rehearsal. And I'm now only working the lunch shift at Hurley's and helping with morning prep, so my afternoons and evenings are free to spend with Phoebe and help her get settled."

He glanced at where Phoebe stood with her group. She was reciting her lines with another girl, her eyes bright. "She looks very happy."

"So far, so good," Clementine said. "She's met the whole family and was so sweet with Lucy, my sister Annabel's stepdaughter. It's only been two days and she's a little standoffish with me, but that's to be expected."

Standoffish? He didn't get that vibe from Phoebe, but then again, he wasn't her foster mother. To Phoebe, he was Logan Grainger, rodeo star. And someone her stepfather, a man she'd admired, had talked up.

"So would tomorrow work?" Clementine asked. "An icebreaker would definitely help."

Icebreaker. He glanced at Clementine and now could see a bit of strain in her features. Maybe the transition period wasn't so smooth?

"Is everything all right?" he whispered. "Has it been tough?"

"Not tough, no," she whispered back. "It's just a little different than I thought it would be, I guess. I mean, I didn't expect Phoebe to treat me like a mom, exactly. Or maybe I did." She shook her head.

"Two days is nothing," he said. "Of course she's going to be hanging back. She'll come around." He remembered those early days when the twins had just lost their parents, how confused they'd been about where

Mommy and Daddy were, why Uncle Logan was living in their house. They hadn't understood at first, then had and they'd gone quiet for what felt like weeks until they started bouncing back. Logan had a feeling Phoebe needed that same adjustment period. Change was change and it could be hard.

She bit her lip. "I hope so. You know when you can just feel someone keeping you at a distance? When they don't quite keep eye contact, don't answer questions beyond yes or no, that kind of thing? That's what Phoebe does with me. She's much more forthcoming with others, though, I noticed. Like when my sister Georgia asked her about Tuckerville, she went on and on, but when I asked her a question earlier, she barely answered."

"Maybe because you're *it*," he said. "The foster mother. Like Mrs. Nivens. Someone with a lot of say in what her life will be like, whether she stays. She's probably just being very cautious."

Clementine nodded, her eyes a bit troubled. "I think that must be it. Her caseworker had warned me not to expect her to jump into my arms with hugs and mother-daughter hair-braiding or whatever. But I didn't expect the distance when she's so friendly and warm with others. I guess I have to give it time."

"Yes," he said. "Once she sees how kind and giving you are, she'll warm up." He took her hand and squeezed it in solidarity, and when she looked up at him in surprise, he was consumed by the urge to hug her close.

Dammit. "Clementine, follow me." He took her by the hand and led her out of the room.

"Where are we going?"

"Over here," he said, leading her into a short, deserted hallway. "You need a hug and I can't exactly hug you in front of all those kids unless you want giggling to interrupt singing and running through lines." He put his arms around her. "It's going to be okay, Clem. Really. You're a natural mother. I've seen you in action with the twins. With the kids here."

"Then why do I feel so awkward?" she asked. "I'm trying, but everything I'm trying isn't working. There's nothing worse than the blank stare."

"Agreed. But it's been two days. She'll come around. She just needs to know you're a keeper, Clem. That's *she's* a keeper."

He could see tears welling in her pretty brown eyes. "Thank you, Logan. *Thank you.* You are absolutely right. And you have no idea how much I needed a hug right then, strong arms around me."

He tilted her chin up with a finger. "I did know, actually."

She smiled. "I suppose so." She wrapped her arms around him and pressed her head against his chest and he just held her for a few moments.

And once again, he had to ask himself just what in tarnation he thought he was doing. Did he not just settle something with himself about avoiding her? Then again, if he was going to let Phoebe meet Crazy Joe, he couldn't avoid Clementine. They were a set now, a package deal.

"I guess I'll see you both tomorrow after school," he said, finally releasing her from the hug and taking a step back.

She cleared her throat and tucked a long swath of dark hair behind her ear, revealing a gold-and-ruby earring. "Phoebe's school lets out at 3:10, so we'll be over by 3:30."

"I'll walk you back in," he said as she led the way to the community room. She smiled at him at the door. "See you tomorrow," he said and turned to leave.

He glanced over at where the twins had been sitting, but they'd moved to the stage. His gaze caught on Phoebe with her group and her face lit up and she waved excitedly.

He waved back, that same unease crawling up his spine. This wasn't what he wanted at all. He was the one who wanted—needed—the distance. Now Phoebe was coming over tomorrow, on his turf, and Clementine was bringing her. The two people on earth with the power to unravel him after he'd worked so hard to wind himself back up in a tight ball.

Chapter Seven

Clementine had been a foster mother for three days. Every time she looked at Phoebe she wanted to hug her. But every time Phoebe looked at her there was this little element of…mistrust? Clementine wasn't sure what the right word was. The girl was definitely distant with her, though. She didn't want Clementine's help with her homework on Monday. She didn't want to help Clementine set up the dining room for lunch, but she'd jumped at the chance to help Annabel marinade chicken breasts and help clean her station, and she'd asked Georgia if she could teach her how to make a lemon tart, her favorite, then had scrubbed the baking station spotless.

It was only Clementine she didn't want to be around. Or get close to.

"It'll take time," Gram said, patting Clementine's

hand as they sat in the kitchen at the round table by the window, taking a tea break after the lunch cleanup on Tuesday.

Clementine hated when her expressions gave her away. But then again, her gram could always read her. It was just after three o'clock. Phoebe had come racing off the school bus a moment ago, saw Daisy, Annabel's beagle, in the yard with Annabel after a trip to the nearby vet, and was delighted by a fetch game. The dog raised her head and let out a howling bay and Phoebe did the same, eliciting some stares from passersby across the street. Clementine smiled. She wanted to rush out and ask Phoebe how her day had gone, if she had a lot of homework, if she'd made a new friend at school. But Phoebe looked so happy out there that Clementine stayed put. She was a little afraid that if she went outside to greet Phoebe, the girl would lose her smile.

This wasn't exactly how Clementine had been expecting this to go. But hadn't she herself been slow to warm up when the Hurleys had first fostered her? Her parents and her sisters had been so nice and welcoming and Clementine could well remember being suspicious of them and hanging back, afraid to let herself like them too much. *Love* them.

"We could think about getting a dog of our own," Gram said, sipping her tea. "A Hurley's mascot. Phoebe could pick one out."

"Really?" Clementine said. "That's a great idea."

"Remember Dumpling?" Gram asked. "That sweet cat adored you when you came to live with your mom and dad."

Clementine remembered. The orange tabby would settle herself down against Clementine wherever she was sitting and made her feel loved. After her parents died, the old cat had moved into the Victorian with the orphaned sisters, and Clementine had gotten much comfort from that furry bundle.

Perhaps a dog would work the same comforting magic on Phoebe, help her bond with Clementine too. "I'm going to ask her right now," she said, rushing out the yard.

But the idea fizzled. Phoebe stared at Clementine blankly. "A dog?" She shrugged and went back to playing with Daisy. "I mean, I like dogs, but I don't know. Is it time to go to Logan's?" she asked, her expression brightening.

Annabel offered Clementine a look of commiseration, then turned to Phoebe. "Time for the pooch and me to go pick up Lucy from school. See you soon, Phoebe. Bye, Clem."

"Do you like being called Clem?" Phoebe asked when Annabel and the beagle had left.

Clementine smiled. "Sure. My sisters call me Clem, Clementine, Tiny. Nicknames are usually a term of endearment."

Phoebe knelt down, opened her backpack, took out her Texas Rangers cap and put it on her head, backward. "My mom used to call me Phoebes. Clyde did too sometimes."

"Would you like me to call you Phoebes?" Clementine asked.

"No," the girl said. "Is it time to go to Logan's?"

Clementine's shoulders slumped. Was she just... dissed?

Stop it, she told herself. *Phoebe has been here for just a few days. This is a huge change for her. Stop expecting fairy-tale behavior.* "Phoebe, I'd like to tell you something important."

"Okay..." Phoebe looked around, everywhere but at Clementine.

And Clementine didn't demand her attention. She needed to let Phoebe accept her at her own pace. "I want you to know you can say anything to me. I want you to feel safe here, safe to be yourself, to speak your mind. If something is bothering you, if you feel uncomfortable, if you feel worried, I want you to say so. And if you want to talk about your mom and Clyde or your aunt, I want you to know you can. I'm here to listen, no matter what."

Phoebe stared at the ground. "Okay."

It'll take time had to be Clementine's new mantra. Or she'd crumble. And crumbling was not an option. She'd signed on for this and she was going to do what it took to make Phoebe comfortable with her. The girl clearly wasn't yet. And that was okay.

It'll take time, she assured herself.

The moment Clementine's car pulled to a stop in front of Logan's house, Phoebe came running out, her hair in a low ponytail under her baseball cap.

"Hi, Logan! Thank you so much for letting me come see Crazy Joe!"

Her enthusiasm made him smile. "Sure thing. But I

don't want to disappoint you. He's not really crazy. He's pure sweetness. After he got sick and I nursed him, he mellowed out. He loves pats on his nose."

Phoebe grinned. "I can't wait to meet him." She rattled off the names of several rodeo bulls, a few of whom he had managed to best, and which were the serious buckers. The girl definitely knew her stuff.

Logan watched Clementine slowly come out of her car, slowly walk over, slowly smile. Hmm. Perhaps things were still a bit strained between her and Phoebe.

"Hi, Clementine," he said, tipping his hat at her.

"Hi. Thanks for having us over."

"My pleasure," he said, dragging his gaze away from the pretty sight of her in her light blue sweater and jeans and cowboy boots. He remembered kissing her, touching her, wanting her so fiercely the other night. He blinked hard to force those thoughts away. "Come on. Crazy Joe's out this way."

They headed out to the large pasture, the beautiful weather—low sixties and abundant sunshine—making jackets unnecessary. The big black bull stood in the waning sun, chewing on some hay on the ground, finally used to the idea that no one was about to sling a rope around him and climb on his back in a tiny chute. As they neared the fence, he noticed Clementine smiling sweetly at Crazy Joe. Though she'd always lived right in town, first with her parents, then her grandmother, Blue Gulch was a ranching community and just about everyone had spent time around livestock. Since Clementine had spent so much time on the ranch as a babysitter for his nephews, she was used to very large bulls, even ones who suddenly let out loud snorts, as Crazy Joe just did.

"Is that Crazy Joe?" Phoebe asked, looking from the bull to Logan. "You're right. He doesn't look very crazy. He looks kind of nice."

"He is," Logan said. "You can go up to him and feed him some hay if you want." He saw Clementine flinch like the new mama she was. "It's safe, I assure you."

"I'm not scared of bulls," Phoebe said, barely tossing a glance at Clementine. She returned her attention to Logan and picked up a cluster of hay, stepping closer toward the waist-high wooden fence that separated her from Crazy Joe, her hand gently moving toward the bull's flanks. "Hi, Crazy Joe. I'm Phoebe. I'm gonna be a bull rider one day." Crazy Joe snorted again and lifted his head, and Phoebe laughed. "He agrees!"

Logan chuckled. "I think he does."

Clementine seemed to be hanging back. He knew she was a pro at being around kids of all ages, but the way Phoebe interacted with her was clearly making Clementine unsure of how to approach the girl, whether to burst in as she always did or stay back a little.

Bring her in, he told himself. *She needs your help right now.* "You can feed him too, Clementine. Or pat him on the side."

Clementine's eyes widened and she glanced from the bull to Phoebe to Logan and back to the bull. "You know, I don't think I've ever touched a bull before. I'd like to pet him, though."

"Bulls are so cool," Phoebe said. "Look how awesome Crazy Joe is."

Clementine tentatively reached out a hand and patted Crazy Joe's side, the bull's head lifting up in her direction. "He likes me!"

Phoebe tilted her head. "I think bulls know who's nice and who's not. Like Santa."

Logan caught the look of happy surprise on Clementine's face. Clearly Phoebe thought her foster mother was nice, which she was. So if Phoebe was keeping herself at arm's length from Clementine, it wasn't because she didn't like her foster mother. Honestly, he couldn't imagine anyone not liking Clementine.

You sure acted like it last August, he reminded himself. Which was something he should rehash with Clementine. People, kids included, acted in all kinds of ways for all kinds of reasons and it often had nothing to do with the person on the receiving end. He knew if he told her not to take it personally she'd slump her shoulders and he got that; how could you not take something personally when it was you on the receiving end of the cold shoulder? But the thing was, oftentimes, that cold shoulder wasn't about you so much as it was about the person giving it.

"Well, I think Crazy Joe is pretty nice himself," Clementine said. "So he used to be a rodeo bull?"

"Logan didn't win on him, but he bested lots of others," Phoebe said. "Isn't it super nice of Logan to let Crazy Joe live here when he didn't last eight seconds on him? He obviously treats Crazy Joe like a king. He has this big pasture and bull friends and all that hay," she added, pointing to the trough near the barn.

"Well, now that you mention it, that does sound super

nice," Clementine said, smiling at Logan. She patted Crazy Joe's side again. "Logan knows you didn't mean to make him lose the event—you were just being a bull, weren't you, Crazy Joe? Doing your thing."

Huh. Talk about not taking something personally, he thought, remembering the last time he'd ridden Joe and gotten thrown hard on his side, his biggest rival walking away with the purse. At least Logan could say he practiced what he preached, when it came to bulls, anyway.

"Yeah, Crazy Joe," Phoebe said, biting her lip. "You were just being a bull." She looked up at Clementine with a sweet expression on her face, and Logan was hopeful that this shared experience and Clementine's wisdom had worked a little magic on their relationship.

"So right now Miss Karen, the twins' sitter, is giving the boys a bath," Logan said, "but she'll be leaving in about five minutes and I promised them 'make your own sundaes.' Would you two like to stay and have some?" Logan asked.

"I love sundaes!" Phoebe said. "Can we?" she asked Clementine.

"I never say no to ice cream sundaes," Clementine said.

That earned her another smile from Phoebe, and they said their goodbyes to Crazy Joe.

They headed in just as Karen was coming down the stairs, the boys racing ahead in front of her, their blond mops damp from their bath. Logan could smell their sweet baby soap from where he stood. Both boys wore blue sweatpants and white T-shirts and their favorite socks with red trucks.

"Yay, it's Phoebe!" Henry said, rushing over.

"Want to see my favorite monster?" Harry asked, holding up a rubber toy with three heads and seven eyes.

"He's awesome," Phoebe said, kneeling down. "I love monster toys."

Logan glanced at Clementine, his turn to be happily surprised. The boys obviously liked Phoebe, having gotten to know her a little from the Christmas show rehearsal. After introducing Karen and Phoebe, the sitter hugged the twins goodbye and left.

A half hour later, ice cream sundaes consumed, Phoebe offered to help the twins practice "Jingle Bells," which morphed into reading a storybook about a little mouse who couldn't find his way home for Christmas. Then they all wanted to play tag, so they went into the backyard, and Logan made coffee for him and Clementine. They sat down on the brown leather couch that faced the sliding glass doors to the backyard, the kids in full view.

"Maybe Phoebe's coming around," Clementine said, her expression wistful as she looked out at Phoebe playing with the twins. "She said I'm nice. Indirectly, anyway. And she seemed to like what I said about a bull just being a bull."

He sipped his coffee. "You *are* nice. And you were very right about the bull thing. A rider just can't take that personally," he threw in, hoping she'd take that nugget for herself.

She nodded, her expression softer. Huh. Who knew that inviting Clyde Parsons's ex-stepdaughter here, which was harder for him than lasting eight seconds on any bull, would lead to so much good for Clementine? He was glad he'd gotten over it and let them come out.

He glanced out at the twins chasing Phoebe, all three of them smiling. "The boys seem to adore her."

"That seems mutual. And she definitely adores you."

He stiffened. And wanted to change the subject. But before he could think of something to ask about rehearsal or what the specials were at Hurley's tomorrow, she added to the subject.

"She has a poster of you up on the wall over her desk," Clementine said. "A rodeo poster. And she keeps Clyde's scrapbook of your rodeo accomplishments on the center of the desk."

He looked away. The rodeo felt like a lifetime ago. "Well, those days are over."

"Do you miss it?" she asked, tucking her legs underneath her. She was slightly facing him now, and he was so aware of her, too aware of her, the scent of her shampoo catching him every now and then.

He leaned his head back against the couch and stared up at the ceiling, shoving his hands in the pockets of his jeans. "Sometimes, more than anything. But most of the time, I hear the crowd chanting Handcuff Cowboy and I want to disappear in a bull chute. I—" He stopped talking and shook his head, grabbing his mug of coffee.

What the heck was wrong with him? Why would he bring that up? There were two sore subjects in his life. Parsons and the Handcuff Cowboy nonsense. And he went and mentioned one of them to someone who knew nothing about it at all. He sat up straight and called himself a fool three times. *Idiot.*

Maybe she wouldn't ask.

"Why would they call you the Handcuff Cowboy?" she asked. Of course she did. "I remember Phoebe mentioning that at our lunch in Tuckerville, but it was clear she didn't know why you were called that."

Thank God, he thought. That wasn't something fit for a kid's ears.

Just tell Clementine and get it over with. Maybe if he told her the cruddy story she'd understand why he was so...prickly on top of everything else.

He sighed and launched into it. "I was headed for the championships and the woman I was dating turned out to be the sister of my biggest rival. She lied about who she was, though. I had no idea she was related to the guy."

He thought of Bethany Appleton, who'd told him her name was Kayla Clark and lied about where she was from, why she was always at the rodeo, why she was dating Logan. How could someone look you right in the eye, kiss you, share such intimate experiences with you and be lying the whole time?

"Oh no," she said. "I don't like where this is going. The sister of your biggest rival?"

He let out a harsh breath and nodded. "I never drink before a championship, for obvious reasons, but one day, before a championship I'd worked hard to prepare for, she spiked the iced tea she made me and the next thing I knew, we were in bed and I was handcuffed to the posts. I was so buzzed I fell asleep. When I woke up, she was nowhere to be found, the championships were long over and I had to call the front desk to help me out. Word leaked. A total embarrassment."

She grimaced and put her mug on the coffee table. "Logan, how awful."

He nodded. "Yeah. She'd dated me only to do exactly what she'd done. Make sure I never made it to the championships so her brother would win and walk away with the purse. That's exactly what happened."

"How the heck could someone do that?" she asked, staring at him. "She…spent time with you only to trick you?"

He nodded, leaning his head back on the couch. "I liked her too. Before that, I mean. I thought she meant everything she said. And every word out of her mouth was a lie."

She shook her head. "All to make sure her brother won the championship. Unbelievable."

"Yup. The day after she came up to me and tried to apologize, to tell me she really did like me and that it was too bad I had to be her big brother's biggest rival, but family was family."

"Wow," Clementine said. "Some apology. I hope she got hers—comeuppance, I mean."

He shrugged. "I never said anything about her. I trusted her and I got burned. I just wanted to forget it and try to get back my standing in the rodeo and live down the whole thing."

"Did you?"

He thought back to those days right after he unintentionally forfeited the championships, some of the worst of his life. "Well, the crowds would chant out

'Handcuff Cowboy' and it'd distract me. I never won another rodeo. Then a few weeks later I got the call from the Blue Gulch police about my brother and his wife. Nothing really mattered after that."

She reached a hand over and touched his arm. "I know."

"You do, don't you?" he said, putting a hand over hers, holding her gaze for a moment. He leaned closer, dying to kiss her, to let his whole conversation fall away.

For a few moments, they both watched the kids playing, Phoebe clearly being purposely slow as she "chased" the boys in a game of tag, the twins shrieking with delight as she neared one of them, only to "miss" them. He relaxed, appreciating how sweet the girl was being with Harry and Henry. He took a sip of his coffee, all thoughts of the rodeo and The Liar and a former life receding.

"Do you plan to tell Phoebe that you're Clyde's biological son?" Clementine asked, and she might as well have poked him with a cattle prod. What the heck? Parsons hadn't even been on his mind for once.

"I don't know," he said, shifting so that her hand moved off his arm.

She bit her lip. "I just wonder if the more time that goes by, the stranger it'll be that you're not telling her."

"I said I don't know, Clementine," he repeated maybe a little too gruffly.

The hand was back on his arm. "I'm sorry. I'm not trying to push you into something." She shook her head. "Now that Phoebe is here, my foster daughter, I guess

I'm hoping you'll start seeing her as just Phoebe, not as Clyde Parsons's stepdaughter."

How could he do that? She was Parsons's stepdaughter and a constant reminder to him of a man he wanted to pretend didn't exist.

"Well, how would telling her that *not* make it even more crystal clear to me that she *is* Parsons's stepdaughter?" he asked. "Right now, I can almost forget because she has no idea."

"I guess I was thinking that once it's out in the open and not a secret being kept, it stops having magnitude for you. It stops being something you need to do something about. You'll be able to look at her as just Phoebe, *my* foster daughter instead of someone so connected to Clyde Parsons."

Oh heck, maybe she was right. He just didn't want to deal with, not yet. "I—"

The sliding glass door opened and the kids rushed in, laughing and talking a mile a minute, and very effectively forcing a change of subject. They headed over to the pile of blocks, Phoebe helping stack them and the boys zooming into them, crashing onto the playmat. Logan glanced at his watch. It was close to six thirty.

"Well, I guess I'd better get these two ready for bed," Logan said, standing up. Ending this conversation. Ending this day.

"Aww," Harry complained.

"Can't we stay up longer and play with Phoebe?" Henry asked.

"Sorry, guys," Logan said, scooping up Harry and flying him horizontally, one of Harry's favorite moves.

He put the boy down and picked up Henry, tossing him up a few inches and catching him, then setting him down.

"I loved being here today," Phoebe said, her hazel eyes so full of happiness he had to take a step back.

"I'm glad," he said. He wanted to add *you're welcome anytime*, but he didn't want to say that before he meant it. And right now, he just wasn't there yet.

"Logan, I know I'm just nine," she said, "but maybe I could do some chores for you around the ranch or help babysit the twins? I could help take care of Crazy Joe. I just love him so much."

What? No. No, no, no. Clementine had brought up the idea of Phoebe spending time on the ranch when they'd first discovered Phoebe existed, but he'd put the idea out of his head. Now here was Phoebe, asking straight out. "You mean like a job?" he said, needing to give himself time to process this.

She nodded. "Well, chores. I need to earn money for something important."

She was looking down at the floor and it was clear she didn't want to be asked for what. He glanced over at Clementine, whose expression seemed…anxious.

Dammit. He didn't want Phoebe hanging around his ranch, reminding him he wasn't a Grainger, that a man named Clyde Turnbull Parsons was his biological father, that he stuffed a PO box full of child support over the first eighteen years of Logan's life, that he went to his rodeos and kept a scrapbook, that he'd taken on the responsibility of a girl with nowhere to go. She'd naturally start talking about her late stepfather and Logan would

have to listen and politely respond and then what? He'd
have to tell her he was Parsons's son, making it very
real, putting it out there, speaking it aloud. He'd learn
all kinds of things about Parsons that he didn't want to
know. Like anything about the man who'd betrayed his
mother and walked out on him before he was even born.

But worse, Phoebe would feel even more connected
to Logan. He wouldn't just be her rodeo hero. He'd be
the son of the man who'd meant more to Phoebe than
anyone, the one person in her young life who apparently hadn't let her down. From the moment Phoebe
knew, Logan would be Parsons's son to her. He didn't
want to be that. Ever.

"I'll work real hard," Phoebe said, staring at Logan
with such hope that his shoulders knotted. "I promise."

Oh hell. He ran a hand through his hair.

"Phoebe, this is a really busy time on Logan's ranch,"
Clementine said, and he appreciated that she was trying to save him, buy him time. "I don't think he has the
hours in the day to supervise a young ranch hand. But I'll
bet my sister Annabel's husband, West, could use some
help at his ranch. Wait till you meet their ponies—" The
dejected look on Phoebe's face interrupted Clementine
and she bit her lip.

"Okay," Phoebe said, staring at her sneakers.

He glanced at Clementine, who looked miserable.
He glanced at Phoebe, who looked even more miserable. But neither looked as miserable as he felt. "Well,
I'll tell you what, Phoebe. Let me look at my schedule
and talk to Clementine about it. Maybe we can figure
something out."

Note the word maybe. *Please, both of you, take careful note of* maybe.

The new look on Phoebe's face could only be described as kid-unwrapping-big-Christmas-present. "Awesome!" Phoebe said, smiling at him. She rushed over to the blocks area, put them away in their bins in seconds flat, straightened out the mat, then hugged each twin. "See you two at the next rehearsal. And remember, it's one-horse open *sleigh*."

The boys hugged her back and suddenly, Phoebe and Clementine were heading to the door. He needed that door to close behind them, needed to be back to his life with the boys.

"Maybe you'll talk to Clementine about it in the morning?" Phoebe asked. "I mean, if you have time."

Maybe, maybe, maybe. Used to be such a nice noncommittal word.

He glanced at Clementine. "I'll make time," he said, surprising even himself. Had he meant to say that? He could have easily said he'd be busy leading the cattle out farther in the morning, then had ranch chores and another area of fence to mend and a ranchers association meeting later in the day. But Phoebe was getting under his skin, just like she'd gotten under Clementine's.

As Clementine offered him a wobbly smile with a thank-you hovering in the air between them, he nodded, again wondering what had happened to his life.

At almost midnight, Clementine couldn't sleep so threw the quilt off and padded downstairs to the second floor. She poked her head in Phoebe's room, the slice of moonlight illuminating the area near Phoebe's bed enough for Clementine to see the girl sleeping peacefully. The scrapbook of Logan's rodeo events was under her arm.

Clementine's heart pinged in her chest. *Oh, Phoebe.* When she'd tucked the girl in earlier, she hadn't had the scrapbook, which meant Phoebe hadn't been able to sleep either and had gotten up for it. Clementine wondered if Phoebe had been reading it or if it just worked like a treasured stuffed animal to make her feel safe as she tried to drift off.

Phoebe's long sandy-brown hair was over her cheek and Clementine wanted to tiptoe in and brush it back, but she was afraid to wake Phoebe. And get caught. Phoebe might think she was "nice," but she was still keeping a distance between them and Clementine knew she had to respect that.

Earlier this evening, at dinner with Gram in the family dining room on the other side of the kitchen, Clementine had asked Phoebe about school and her favorite subject and what her favorite things to do were. Phoebe answered her politely enough in one or two words, but all the girl wanted to talk about was her rodeo hero, Logan Grainger, and his ranch, excitedly telling Essie all about Crazy Joe and how she got to pet him and that maybe she'd get to do some chores around the ranch for some spending money. Essie Hurley had grown up on a ranch, so she and Phoebe had tons to talk about, and Gram had tried her darnedest to bring Clementine into the conversation, but once again, Phoebe kept her at arm's length.

It'll take time, she said to herself, repeated her mantra.

As she watched Phoebe sleep, she wondered what she wanted to earn money for. *Something important*, the girl had said. Maybe Phoebe would tell Logan what it was. If he agreed to let her do some chores at the ranch.

She popped her head out and went downstairs, careful not to wake her grandmother, whose room was on the first floor. Essie Hurley was a light sleeper. In the kitchen, Clementine considered working on perfecting her Creole sauce; she was so close to getting it just right, but the aroma would definitely wake up Gram and might drift upstairs too. Maybe a midnight snack, something to do, something to settle the slightly acidic feeling churning in her belly and up her throat. She settled for a peanut butter and honey sandwich on a biscuit.

She was suddenly struck by a memory, of Charlaine Hurley, her dear mother, making her this exact midnight snack in those early days when she'd first brought Clementine to live with her. Charlaine had lovely auburn hair, much like Annabel's, and beautiful green eyes like Georgia's, and Clementine had been so afraid of what she felt inside that she clammed up around Charlaine. Her mother had been so kind and patient, filling eight-year-old Clementine's silences with stories about Charlaine's mother-in-law, Essie Hurley, who'd taught her how to make her famed biscuits but Charlaine knew hers didn't live up to the master's. Clementine remembered thinking her new foster mother's biscuits were the best thing she'd ever tasted in her life. She remembered wanting to say that, how it was bursting out of her chest, but she couldn't get her lips to form the words, to find her voice. So she'd started crying, and Charlaine had just held her, probably wondering what on earth she'd said that had made her cry.

Time, Clementine knew from experience. *Just let it happen. Don't push, don't rush. And don't be envious of that closeness she has with Logan, with Gram and your sisters already. Be grateful for it.*

Why was everything easier said than done? She poured herself a little iced tea, then cleaned up and moved over to a chair by the window, staring outside at the stars dotting the dark sky. She caught on one and made a wish in just a word: *please.*

Finally, she went back upstairs and got into bed. Her phone on her bedside table was glowing, which meant she missed a text, call or email.

A text. From Logan.

Tomorrow after school would be okay for Phoebe to start "work." Once a week, $10.

Her heart lifted and she texted back, She'll be over the moon. Thank you.—C

There was a couple of minutes' delay, then he texted. Good night.—L

Glad for Phoebe, Clementine flopped over onto her stomach, thinking she'd be able to fall right asleep, but then tossed and turned, tossed and turned, rearranging the pillows, her mind now on everything Logan had told her earlier about the awful woman who'd lied to him. She tried to imagine Logan, the man she knew, alone in a hotel room before a rodeo, trying to live down that silly moniker, dealing with the betrayal from a woman he'd cared about and getting that terrible phone call from the police about the loss of his brother and sister-in-law. No wonder he'd been so slow to do something about their obvious attraction earlier this year. He'd been burned, embarrassed, and then Clementine had entered his life as his sons' new sitter, and it made sense that he'd been cautious about their obvious attraction. And then he'd finally, finally, finally kissed her after months, and wham, the letter had whacked him upside the head again.

He is doing what he thinks is right, even if it doesn't feel *right,* she realized. That wasn't easy. And it made her love him even more.

There was just no sense in trying to deny it anymore, to keep the word out of her head where Logan was concerned. She did love him, deeply, even if she knew heartache was what she'd get in return. She knew he had feelings for her, maybe even strong feelings, but who knew what those feelings were really about. Attraction, yes. Gratitude at how she'd cared for his twins back when she'd been their sitter. Appreciation that he could talk to her about the things that were tearing him up. All that combined to make strong feelings. Not love. If he'd been in love with her back in August when he'd gotten Parsons's letter, wouldn't love had won out? He wouldn't have been able to distance himself, avoid her. Right?

His ability to trust had been blown to bits, she reminded herself. Of course he'd push her away.

But then again, if he'd loved her, maybe he would have drawn her closer, needed her.

Clementine flopped onto her stomach and punched her pillow to make it more comfortable but it felt like mush and concrete at the same time. Or was that just her head?

Stop going over it, she told herself. He'd been gobsmacked and shocked and had his world turned upside down and he couldn't deal with anything else, couldn't trust. That made sense, no matter what his feelings were or weren't for her.

She didn't know whether to hang on to hope or let go of it.

Hang on, she told herself. *Just like you're doing with Phoebe.* Logan had gone from a shut door to inviting her in; that was something. There were still miles of distance between them too, but at least he'd opened the darned door. *If he closes it again, then you'll call yourself a fool, wise the heck up and focus on your foster daughter and your life and not your dumb heart.*

Her weary brain felt better and she pulled the quilt up and felt herself drifting off, Logan's gorgeous face managing to lull her to sleep.

Chapter Eight

After Logan saw the twins off to school in the morning, he did the barn chores he usually delegated to his ranch hand, cleaning out the stalls, hoping to work out some of the tight muscles that had settled into his shoulders and back and arms and legs overnight. Phoebe hanging around his ranch. A walking, talking, breathing reminder that he had a biological father he wanted to forget.

Logan hosed down the last stall, then walked out into the December sunshine to the horses' pasture and tossed a few apple slices to the horses and ponies. He watched them graze for a while, but he kept thinking of Phoebe, imagining her sitting next to Parsons at a rodeo, excitedly eating her popcorn and clapping for him. He hated the thought of Clyde Parsons in the stands, watching him, thinking they were related, that there was anything to their connection other than DNA.

As if DNA didn't matter at all. It did and didn't. DNA wasn't everything, but it wasn't "nothing," either.

A father showed up. A father cared. A father took responsibility. A father raised you. That was what a father was. Parsons was just a man who'd walked away and was never seen again.

But not *unheard from* again. Unfortunately? Logan had spent many nights tossing and turning over that one. Was ignorance bliss? If you had no cause to wonder about something, than yeah, ignorance sure as hell was blissful.

He had to get out of his head, focus on the physical labor and not think so much. He'd take Sundappled up to the area of fence that needed repairing, then ride along and check the rest of the fencing, maybe take off hard for a bit, give Sundappled a workout.

But first, he needed coffee. Strong coffee to clear his mind.

He went back inside the house to put a pot on, then remembered he'd used the last of the coffee at dawn when he'd gotten up. He needed a big mug of strong coffee. Which meant a trip into town. He opened the refrigerator and took a quick inventory of what else he needed from the grocery store. The twins ate like birds and lately, so did Logan, but he saw he was low on cheese for their beloved grilled cheese sandwiches and the Western omelets he liked to make himself in the early mornings. The bread was nearly gone too.

He'd drive into town to the grocery store, then stop at the coffee shop for their biggest size cup of dark brew.

The ride did him good. He blasted The Rolling Stones, thinking of nothing but Mick Jagger's voice and the song lyrics, and there was nothing like grabbing a cart and heading into the grocery store to numb him. Grocery shopping was a chore, but a necessary one. He consulted his mental list, remembering he needed cold cereal, and swung his cart back to aisle one, his gaze on the sugary, crunchy kiddie cereal he personally loved, but reaching for the healthier oat one for the boys' sake.

"Logan Grainger! How nice to see you."

Logan whirled around at the familiar voice. Delia Cooper, who'd been his mother's friend. His mother had been gone for almost ten years, but the Coopers had come by often in the first weeks after Logan had come home to raise the twins. He and the boys were all that was left of the once much bigger Grainger family. She held out her arms for a hug and Logan stepped in, the woman wrapping her arms tightly around him.

"How are those adorable nephews of yours?" she asked.

"They're doing great. They'll be in the Christmas show this year."

Delia smiled. He liked that she hadn't changed in all the years he'd known her; she had the same short blond hairstyle and wore a red sweater with a big embroidered reindeer on it. "Well, I won't miss that."

The Graingers and the Coopers had lived next door to each other on small neighboring ranches. The Coopers' children were older, but they'd played with Logan and his brother sometimes. His mother had been a private woman, more introverted than his more social father. But many times Logan would find Ellie Grainger sitting or walking with Delia.

Would his mother have confided in Delia? No way. Delia Cooper was too chatty and the truth way too personal. Back when he'd first received Parsons's bombshell of a letter and he hadn't been sure if what Parsons revealed was true or not, Logan had tried to think of anyone who'd been close to his mother in those days. But there was no one, really. Delia was a neighbor and a friend, but would his mother have told anyone if she wasn't planning on ever telling Logan himself?

Ask her. Just bring it up and see how she reacts.

He cleared his throat. "Delia, a few months ago I received a letter from someone my mother used to know, and I was wondering if the name rings a bell with you. Clyde Parsons."

He stared at her and she didn't disappoint. Her expression changed so suddenly from warm and open to shocked and guarded.

She knew.

She glanced away at the display of cereal boxes, concern etched on her face.

He took a breath. "I don't want to put you in an uncomfortable position of talking about something you were very likely asked never to breathe a word about. But the man wrote me a deathbed confession and I have some questions. Maybe you could answer some."

Delia bit her lip, then glanced at her cart, which so far contained only a box of steel-cut oatmeal. "I'll put this back. Looks like you haven't started on your shopping either. Let's take a walk so we have some privacy."

Logan breathed a sigh of relief that she was willing to talk about it and nodded. He wasn't up for talking about something so personal in the middle of the grocery store either. A couple of weeks ago, he'd stopped in for a few jars of peanut butter, the boys' favorite food, and managed to learn that so-and-so was having an affair and that so-and-so's kid was failing algebra and that so-and-so's sister-in-law couldn't cook to save her life. People sure did like to chat in grocery store aisles. And he didn't want anyone listening in on his and Delia's conversation.

Logan returned both their carts and he and Delia walked out of the store and around back to a large grassy area with a few picnic tables meant for an outside break area for employees. No one was around. Across the field, an elderly woman was walking what looked like a miniature poodle. The woman was far enough way not to be able to overhear them, so Logan felt comfortable staying put. He kept his eyes on the dog, suddenly anxious about facing Delia and whatever information she had.

Delia was watching the scampering dog too, worry in her brown eyes. She seemed uncomfortable.

"I really just have one question, Delia."

She turned to face him. "Okay."

"Did my father know?"

She nodded. "Yes."

Logan almost sagged with relief. He'd had no idea how badly he needed that to be the answer, to know that his father had treated him the way he had, like a flesh-and-blood son, despite knowing. To Logan it meant that his father's love for him had been based in truth, in reality, in love and commitment. Not in "ignorance is bliss." If Delia's answer had been no or I don't know, Logan would have always wondered how his father would have felt *had* he known, if it would have changed things.

Not based on the Haywood Grainger he knew, though. But still, it would have poked at him, the not knowing, the wondering.

"He knew," Logan repeated, relief flooding him.

"He knew," Delia said. "Your parents grew up together in Blue Gulch, as you know, they'd been childhood friends, but never dated. Then one day, your father found your mother, just eighteen years old and newly graduated from high school, sitting and crying on a swing at the playground behind the town hall. She told him the truth, that she'd just found out she was pregnant, barely six weeks along, and that when she told the baby's father he said he was sorry but a settled-down life wasn't the life for him and he was gone in an hour, packed and completely gone. He was a twenty-year-old traveling ranch hand who'd been hired on at your grandparents' place and she'd fallen for him fast."

Logan took that in, trying not to imagine his scared mother going to see the father of her baby after the first rejection and finding him cleared out. Bastard.

"Two minutes after hearing she was pregnant, your father proposed to your mother. He told her he'd secretly loved her his whole life, ever since they were kids, and if she'd have him, he'd take care of her and raise the baby as if it were his own flesh and blood. No one had to know any different, he'd assured her."

Oh, Dad, he thought, tears pricking his eyes at the thought of his gallant father, the best man he knew. He'd gotten the girl he always loved, but he'd taken on another man's child and he had raised Logan as if he was his own son.

"Before you were even born, your father loved you, Logan. He and your mother got married and both sets of parents helped them buy the ranch you grew up on and they settled in to await your birth. By the time you were born, you were Haywood's son. It just was. You were his son same as if you had his DNA. That was what they believed in their hearts and it was their truth."

"But it wasn't the truth," Logan said.

"There was no good reason for you to know, Logan. No good reason then. I'm not sure there's a good reason now."

Phoebe Pike flashed in his mind. If Logan didn't know, if Parsons hadn't sent him that letter, if he hadn't gone looking for information about him, he wouldn't know about Phoebe, a girl who had his rodeo champ poster up above her desk, a girl with losses that made his heart ache when he thought about what she'd been through.

"Deathbed confession, you said?" Delia continued. "Selfish to the end. He wanted to go in peace, I suppose, apologizing for old wrongs. But what good does knowing do you? Why'd he have to put this all in your head and make you question your identity and your father?"

Ignorance *was* bliss, Logan knew. But the truth was the truth, no ways around it. Good or bad, pretty or ugly, the truth was about acceptance and facing facts. Logan had been unwilling to do that when he first got Parsons's letter. He didn't feel all that much closer to doing so, either.

But another truth was that his father, Haywood Grainger, had loved him before he was born and had decided that he was Logan's father, no ifs, ands or buts. Haywood became Logan's father that moment on the swings when he proposed marriage, proposed a future.

Logan liked that truth. It filled in a lot of raw cracks in his heart. And for that, he was grateful.

"Thank you for telling me about my parents," he said. "It means a lot to know my dad knew and that it didn't matter that I wasn't biologically his. He never treated me any differently than my brother."

"You are his son, Logan. He was your father. Nothing will change that. Not a letter from Clyde, not DNA, nothing."

He nodded, liking her surety.

"If you have more questions, you can always ask," she said. "I'm the only person besides both sets of your grandparents who ever knew the truth. Your mother insisted on sitting down her parents and Haywood's and telling them. She didn't like the idea of anyone thinking that Haywood had proposed because he'd gotten her pregnant. She wanted them to know he proposed because he was a good man and because he loved her."

Sounded like his mother. He smiled at the thought of her doing what she thought was right. Both sets of grandparents were long gone, but the Graingers had always treated him the same as his young brother.

"Thank you, Delia," he said. "You've helped me feel a lot better about the whole crazy thing."

Delia hugged him, then headed back around the corner to finish her shopping, and Logan stayed put, watching two other dogs playing on the far side of the expanse of grass. He'd liked what he heard about his parents, about his father, about his grandparents. But the jury was still out on what kind of man Clyde Parsons was. Why had he bothered with the letter? Had it been just to appease his guilt? Maybe he thought Logan already knew, that his mother had told him long ago. He didn't get that sense from the letter, though.

He wanted that question answered, but there was only one person on earth who knew anything about Clyde Parsons, and Logan wasn't about to poke around in the memory of a foster kid to get those answers. Phoebe clearly didn't know he was Parsons's biological son. But she could help him fill in the gaps of what kind of person he'd been.

Thing was, Logan still wasn't sure he wanted to know. Maybe Parsons had changed from the twenty-year-old ranch hand who'd walked out on his pregnant girlfriend. Wasn't Phoebe proof of that? Problem was that acknowledging Parsons as his biological father meant accepting that the great Haywood Grainger wasn't. And Logan just couldn't do that. No way.

He sighed and watched the little dogs chase each other. Phoebe was coming over after school to "work" to earn some money and learn about running a ranch.

Maybe he should just get it out in the open, explain his connection to her other than rodeo hero.

He looked up at the blue sky, following a giant fluffy cloud moving westward. No answers there either.

Clementine loaded up her tray with the McDowells's lunches, the blackened chicken po'boy special, the fish and chips, and a big side of spicy sweet potato fries. She glanced at her watch. Almost two o'clock. The lunch rush at Hurley's Homestyle Kitchen had slowed down; only two tables were filled. She was desperately in need of a long, hot shower before taking Phoebe over to Logan's. This morning, after walking Phoebe to the elementary school as she did each morning, she'd come back and helped out in the kitchen since the bigwigs from Texas Trust had their annual holiday lunch at Hurley's today. The luncheon featured po'boys of every kind and every imagined side dish, from fried green tomatoes to Gram's famous loaded twice-baked potatoes. Then a waitress had called in sick and Clementine had worked double duty, which was usually no problem since she could practically do her job in her sleep and do it well. But today, she had a lot on her mind.

Just when she'd thought Phoebe was letting her in a little, the distance was back. This morning, Phoebe had been staring in the mirror on her closet door, and Clementine had told her she looked great, which apparently had been the wrong thing to say.

"I don't look great," Phoebe said. "Emily Catwaller said I look like a boy and that if I didn't have long hair, she'd think I was one."

Clementine knew the Catwallers. Every time the family, including Emily, a fellow fourth-grader, came into Hurley's, they sent at least one dish back since it wasn't "prepared to exact specifications" and Donald Catwaller, a lawyer, always had loud conversations on his cell phone. Once Essie had asked him to take his phone outside and he'd humphed at her. The family had thankfully stopped coming in for months, but Hurley's food was irresistible and unfortunately, the Catwallers were back often.

"Do you like the way you dress?" Clementine had asked Phoebe.

"It's how I dress," Phoebe said, looking in the mirror at her blue T-shirt with another Stocktown Rodeo advertisement and her slim blue jeans and baseball cap. "It's how I've always dressed. I don't like skirts and pink and frilly stuff."

"Then that's all that matters," Clementine said with a smile. "It's your style."

Phoebe shrugged. "But *should* I wear something pink and frilly so I'd fit in better? My stepfather once bought me a pink sweater with little unicorns on it as a joke." She smiled. "We cracked up over it." Her smile faltered. "Maybe I *should* wear that to school."

"You wear what you like," Clementine said. "You are who you are, right? And that is someone pretty great."

Phoebe glanced at Clementine, then down at her feet, at her usual orange sneakers. She slid open the closet door and rummaged around, then pulled out a pink sweater. With little unicorns all over it. "Maybe next

Halloween," she said, holding it up and giggling. "If it still fits."

Clementine laughed. "Yeah, that doesn't look like you. It sure is cute, though."

"Clyde loved it," Phoebe said, the wistful expression back. "The day he told me he was really sick, I wore it to the dinner table that night and he started crying. At first I thought I made him upset, but he explained to me that I'd made him very happy because 'even though it's the dumbest sweater on earth,' I wore it because he gave it to me, because I cared about him."

"That's a beautiful memory, Phoebe." She stepped closer, wanting to give the girl a big hug, just hold her and let her cry if she wanted to, but Phoebe stepped back and then Clementine had frozen.

"I'd better get to school," Phoebe had said, quickly putting the sweater back on the row of shelves above the rod. Then she'd given herself a harsh glance in the mirror and turned away, insecurity in her sweet hazel eyes.

Again, Clementine had stepped forward, determined to hug Phoebe and give the girl what she didn't even know she wanted most of all—love, assurance, security. But Phoebe had walked around her and headed for her backpack near the door, a wall of distance erected between them as though it was made of brick.

Time, Clementine told herself for the thousandth time as she glanced around the almost empty dining room's tables and refilled the Cantor sisters' coffee mugs.

Then there was the matter of Logan on her mind. She'd gone to sleep thinking of him; she'd woken up thinking of him.

And in an hour she was due at his ranch, a piece of her heart staying behind with him every time she was near him.

"Thank for you letting her come here," Clementine said to Logan as they watched Phoebe reach out toward Lulu with an apple slice in her a hand. The mare took it and Phoebe grinned. Then she gave Winnie and the other ponies their snacks and used the brush to groom them the way he'd showed her during her fifteen-minute tutorial.

They sat at the picnic table near the pony pasture, both on the same side so they could watch Phoebe and so Logan could rush over if anything went wrong. He was ostensibly buffing a saddle on the table, but he was really keeping a close eye on his young "ranch hand," as was Clementine.

"She's earning her ten dollars, that's for sure," Logan said, smiling at how carefully Phoebe ran the grooming brush down Winnie's side, gently patting the pony's nose and telling the little horse she was being a very good girl. "How are things going at home?"

Clementine shrugged. "Step forward and back, repeat, repeat. I know from my own experience that this is how it can go. But I just want to rush straight to love and hugs and hair-brushing and long walks."

"You'll get there," he assured her.

She nodded, and he hoped she believed him. "You're doing a great job with Winnie," Clementine called out.

Phoebe turned and smiled. "I love grooming the ponies. I love everything about ranch life."

"Me too," Logan called out, "but I sure would love to live in a restaurant. Waking up to the smell of biscuits. Having a smothered po'boy anytime I want."

He did mean that; he'd be very happy to have a Hurley's biscuit slathered in apple butter just a staircase away every morning and coffee break, but he'd said it for Clementine's sake. He felt her looking at him, and her expression made it clear he'd surprised her. Because he'd been kind? She had to know how much he cared about her. Didn't she?

Maybe it was better if she didn't.

"It's awesome," Phoebe said. "Georgia, that's Clementine's sister, taught me how to make biscuits yesterday. She even gave me enough to bring in for my class today. Now almost everyone likes me."

Logan paused in buffing the saddle. "I'm sure everyone liked you before that too. I mean, you're very likeable." He smiled at her, but the expression on Phoebe's face suddenly had his own faltering.

"Emily Catwaller called me 'foster kid' today," Phoebe said, her eyes on her sneakers. "'Don't let the foster kid touch you or you'll turn into one,' she said at recess today. Some kids stuck up for me, but some backed away. Whatever. I totally get it. Who'd want to be a foster kid?" She was still staring at her feet and clearly trying not to cry.

Logan shook his head. Why were there always mean kids? Why the hell couldn't everyone just be kind to one another?

Clementine gave Logan an uneasy glance, then stood up and walked over to the fence. "There are all kinds of families in this world," she said, her expression tight. "I dealt with those kinds of taunts too when I was in foster care. It hurts."

"Did you kick someone?" Phoebe asked. "I wanted to kick Emily."

"I wanted to also," Clementine said. "I didn't, though, 'cause I'd get in trouble for that. And because striking back that way isn't the answer—it'll never make you feel better, even if it seems like some kind of justice at the time."

"So what *is* the answer?" Phoebe asked, staring at Clementine.

Logan wasn't sure if he should go inside to give them some privacy, but heck, he too wanted to know the answer. He pretended to be working hard on buffing the saddle, but his ears were glued to the conversation at the fence.

Clementine glanced at the pony, then back at Phoebe. "Well, when some kids were taunting me about being a foster kid, I thought to myself, well, I *am*. I *am* a foster kid. That's just the way it is. And I could either get all upset or I could just accept the truth and figure out a way to make myself happy. I used to make lists titled Clementine Is and then wrote down all the things I thought I was. Foster kid was on the list but so was smart and determined and a fast runner and a good listener and a big reader and a nice person. It might sound weird to make a list about yourself, but it helped me really think about who I actually was. Foster kid was pretty far down the list. It was just one thing about me. Not everything."

Logan had long paused with the buffing cloth. He stared at Clementine, vaguely noting the way the sunshine lit her dark hair and the side of her face. All she said seemed to flow right inside him, in his veins, in his bones.

Foster kid was pretty far down the list. It was just one thing about me. Not everything.

If he could make this cruddy truth about Parsons just one thing instead of everything, he'd be a hell of lot happier. But he couldn't seem to.

Phoebe bit her lip and glanced at Clementine, then at the pony. But she didn't say anything for a moment. "Well, I don't like the truth," she finally shouted, hugging the grooming brush to her chest. "The truth stinks!" she yelled and then went running to the far side of the pasture, stopping at the fence and sliding down onto her bottom, her knees up and her face in her hands despite the fact that she still held on to that grooming brush. Logan could see her slight body trembling, her shoulders heaving her sobs.

Logan got up and walked over to Clementine, who looked absolutely miserable.

"I thought I was saying the right thing but lately, I get everything wrong," Clementine said, shaking her head.

"No. You said just the right thing. She's just a kid, but she has a lot to cope with and she does need to learn how to deal with it all so that it doesn't take over who she is. That's not easy. It's not easy for a grown-up, either."

"I know," Clementine said softly. She reached out

and squeezed his hand as if in thanks, then started heading for the fence gate to go after Phoebe.

"Clem, wait. Let me talk to her."

If anyone knew how the truth could stink, he did. And maybe it was time to tell Phoebe that he'd been hit with a hard truth lately, one he'd found impossible to swallow, one that had been wreaking havoc inside him for months.

But how was he going to tell her she shouldn't let her own hard truths wreak havoc with her if he couldn't stop his from tearing him up?

Dammit. Just when he thought he had something to offer Phoebe, something that might help her, he realized he didn't.

"Okay," Clementine said, her voice barely above a whisper. "I just wish I knew what to say, how to make things better for her. I'm supposed to be the one who knows what she's going through."

He reached up a hand to her cheek. "You're doing great, Clementine. I'm not trying to overstep, trust me. You're doing an amazing job as her foster mother. Phoebe is human and only nine and she hasn't even been with you a week. Don't beat yourself up. You're doing your best and your best is amazing."

She gave a wobbly nod, uneasily glancing over at where Phoebe was sitting all huddled up.

"I think it's time I told Phoebe about something that I had to deal with back in August," Logan said, pulling off his Stetson and running a hand through his hair. "And how I haven't dealt with it very well at all."

Clementine gasped. "I guess the right time made itself apparent."

He nodded, setting the hat back on his head. "It sure did." He led the way over and sat down beside Phoebe, patting the spot next to him for Clementine. She sat down beside him, and he squeezed her hand.

The girl's shoulders were still quaking, which meant she was still crying. She took off her baseball cap and set it down next to her, then pushed her hair out of her face and used her sleeve to wipe tears away, still keeping her grip on that grooming brush.

"Phoebe," Logan said, his heart clenching at what he was about to say. "I want to tell you something. I recently had to deal with a difficult situation. Something that tore me up inside."

Phoebe looked up at him and wiped under her eyes again. "You did? What was it?"

He glanced over at Clementine next to him, and the trust in her eyes settled something inside him. It was time to tell Phoebe, even if he didn't have all the answers. He just knew that his own hard truth was tearing him up because he *hadn't* dealt with it. And every day that he didn't, it would consume him more and take over his entire being, his every thought.

He cleared his throat. "Well, back in August, I received a letter out of the clear blue sky from a man telling me that he was my biological father—not the man who raised me, not the man who I always believed was my father."

"Whoa, really?" she said, staring at him. "You must have been freaked-out."

Yup, he thought. *That pretty much nails it.* "I was," he said. "It hit me really hard. I had to deal with the truth about myself and I didn't like it or want any part of it."

"So what happened?" she asked. "It stopped bothering you?"

"Nope. It still bothers me. And I'll be honest, I'm having a hard time accepting it. But do you want to know the one thing that has helped me deal with it?"

Phoebe nodded, her eyes wide. "What?"

"Talking to someone who understands," he said. "Someone who just gets it. Someone who's a good listener."

Phoebe tilted her head. "Who'd you talk to?"

"I talked to Clementine," he said, reaching over and taking Clementine's hand without looking at her. He felt her squeeze his hand back. "And talking to Clementine helped me process everything. Sometimes I'd be really mad and clam up. Sometimes, I'd ramble on, talking in circles. But talking about it really helps. At first, I didn't want to talk about it at all. But then I found I needed to."

Phoebe looked past Logan at Clementine, at their entwined hands. "It was nice of you to listen to Logan."

"I'm glad I was able to," Clementine said. "Everyone needs someone to talk to, to confide in."

"You know what else, Phoebe?" Logan said. "Sometimes you just need someone to listen to you, and sometimes you need to be challenged. Sometimes you really do need someone to say that it might really help if you looked at something a different way than you are. Clementine has a knack for knowing when to do both."

The woman really did. And sometimes, he thought, you don't even realize something until you say it aloud.

Phoebe looked at Clementine again, her eyes wide.

"I want to tell you something else, Phoebe," Logan said. "Something that isn't easy for me. And it has to do with you."

"With me?" Phoebe said, her big hazel eyes curious.

He nodded. *Here goes everything*, he thought. There was no turning back now. Once Phoebe knew, everything would change; they would become…connected in a way he couldn't deny any longer. And he wasn't sure how he'd feel then.

"Phoebe, the letter I received, from the man who told me he was my biological father—that man was Clyde Parsons." He watched her eyes grow even bigger.

Her mouth dropped open. "My Clyde Parsons? My stepdaddy?"

Logan nodded. "He was very sick and knew his time was coming and wanted to make sure I knew the truth. Clementine and I went to Tuckerville to find out some more information about him and that's how we learned about you."

Phoebe stared at him. "So if Clyde was your father, that means you're…like my stepbrother."

Every muscle in his body stiffened. He felt something close up inside him, tighten into a hard knot.

"My stepbrother is Logan Grainger! My hero is my stepbrother!" Phoebe stood up, joy on her face, and she finally let go of the grooming brush. "I can't believe this. You're my stepbrother! I mean, I know that Clyde and I weren't blood-related, but still. It counts, right?"

He felt Clementine's eyes on him. This was the million-dollar question. If he didn't consider himself Clyde Parsons's son, not in a way that did count, did he consider himself Phoebe's stepbrother?

The answer, in his heart, was no. No, no, no. But the truth made the answer a yes. He *was* her stepbrother. And for Phoebe's sake, that was the answer he'd give her. The truth. The truth that he hadn't dealt with, couldn't deal with. He didn't consider Clyde Parsons his father and he never would. DNA didn't make a father. That was also the damned truth.

"Yes," he finally said, standing up. "It counts."

She flung herself into his arms and it took all his doing, but he wrapped her in a hug. He wasn't entirely comfortable with this, but hell, this was how it unfolded.

Clementine stood up with a wobbly smile on her face.

"Wow, Logan Grainger, my stepbrother," Phoebe said again and then spun around once, her smile as bright as the sunshine.

He ignored the knot forming in his shoulders. "Clementine and I both wanted you to know the truth, but I wasn't ready to tell you until now."

"I guess I can understand that," Phoebe said, glancing from Logan to Clementine and back again.

"Well," he said, hoping Clementine would pick up on his cue. "I need to pick up the boys from their sitter in a little while." That was also the truth, but a bigger one was that he needed to be alone right now, needed to digest everything that happened today. He hadn't expected most of it.

Clementine dusted off her jeans. "Perfect timing

since we need to get home for dinner, Phoebe. Gram is making us her special pasta dish, and you don't want to miss that." She glanced at Logan. "Thanks for today," she said, her voice catching.

Before he could blink, Phoebe came charging at him again, wrapping him in a hug.

"See you next week," she said.

"See you next week," he repeated.

It had taken everything inside him to parrot back those words.

Chapter Nine

At dinner all Phoebe could talk about was finding out that her rodeo hero was actually her stepbrother. Phoebe's happiness meant everything to Clementine, but she couldn't help longing for Phoebe to feel even a smidgen of that same enthusiasm for her foster mother. As she pushed around Gram's amazing pasta with prosciutto and peas in pink cream sauce, her appetite gone, Clementine chastised herself for that line of thought; after all the girl had been through, Phoebe deserved all the joy in the world. Clementine fully understood that Logan was a connection to a clearly loving parental figure in Phoebe's life, the only person who'd been there for her, who'd loved and taken care of her. Someone who had taken her to all Logan's events, making Logan as important to her as he must have been to Clyde, in his own way.

Of course Phoebe was even crazier about Logan Grainger than she'd been when he was just her hero. As if there was anything *just* about a hero. But now he'd been elevated to superhero.

She would just have to keep trying to find her way into Phoebe's guarded heart. Thing was, no matter how hard she tried to blast through the barriers the girl kept erecting, she couldn't. During dinner, Phoebe would politely answer Clementine's questions and politely acknowledge a comment she'd made, but there was no gusto in her voice or expression.

After dinner, Essie Hurley, who knew Clementine pretty well, could clearly sense her granddaughter was uneasy and needed some time to herself and asked Phoebe to watch a video with her about the rodeo and explain how things worked. Phoebe had jumped at the chance.

Thankful for dear Gram, Clementine had trudged upstairs and taken a long bubble bath, trying to do what she herself had said had to be done: accept the truth. Phoebe adored and revered Logan, and as her foster mother Clementine needed to be grateful that the girl had someone to feel that way about. Even if it wasn't her. She'd stayed in the bath a long time, the lavender bubbles helping soothe her body and mind, but when she came out, her heart was as heavy as it had been before.

As she tucked Phoebe in for the night, pulling the covers up under her chin, Phoebe said, "This was one of the best days of my life." Then she'd yawned big, twice, and Clementine should see she was exhausted, that the long day of school, chores at the ranch and con-

versations that had taken surprising turns had done a
number on her. She needed to rest.

Clementine kissed her on the forehead and said good-
night, then turned to leave, and at the door, when she
looked back, Phoebe had turned on her side, her eyes
closed, her expression one of absolute contentment, the
scrapbook of Logan's accomplishments peeking out
from underneath her pillow.

A certain peace came over Clementine herself at that
sight. The expression on Phoebe's sweet young face was
the very expression Clementine hoped the girl would
always have. It meant she was happy.

"Good night, sweet girl," she whispered to Phoebe
then quietly left the room. She was thinking about turning in early herself, not that she expected to sleep, when
her phone buzzed with a text from Logan. Phoebe had
left her Texas Rangers cap in the pasture and he'd drop
it by in the morning.

How about I come pick it up now? she texted back.
I could use someone to talk to.

Come on over. I'll put coffee on.—L

Better make it herbal tea. I won't be able to sleep as
it is.

Done.—L.

After Gram assured her it was fine with her for Clementine to leave, that she'd keep an ear on Phoebe,
Clementine drove over to Logan's with a box full of

biscuits and cookies that her grandmother insisted she take. That was her Gram.

He was at the door when she pulled up, waiting for her. He looked so handsome in his navy T-shirt and worn jeans, his feet bare. The sound of a teakettle started to whistle. "There's the water," he said. "I'd better go shut off the burner before it wakes the twins."

She followed him into the kitchen and set down the box of treats on the counter. "You were wonderful today, Logan. How you handled things, what you said, how you said it. I don't know where you got your gift from, but I envy it."

He poured steaming water into the mugs and gave each tea bag a few dunks. She could smell the chamomile from where she stood. "I just said what felt right. I learned that from you."

She burst into tears and he rushed over to her and enveloped her in his arms, letting her cry and just holding her. It felt so good to be in his strong arms, his soapy, masculine scent all around her. She took a deep breath and looked up at him. She loved him so damned much that she lifted up on her toes and kissed him.

He stared at her, his blue eyes intense. "The last time I kissed you, you told me we shouldn't, that it would complicate things. I've worked very, very hard to respect that and not touch you. But if you kiss me again, I can't promise you anything."

She couldn't help the smile that broke through. She knew she was aiding in her own future heartbreak, that Logan Grainger was a lone wolf, as least for the foreseeable future, and that he didn't love her. But she needed to feel his hands on her, wanted him to kiss her, wanted what *he'd* wanted the last time: to be taken away from herself, to be taken out of her life for just a few minutes. So she put her hands on the sides of his face, his late-night stubble sexy against her fingers. Then she tilted her head up and kissed him again. He tightened his hold on her, deepening the kiss and she felt herself melting against him.

"Are you sure?" he asked, trailing a finger from her cheek down her neck and along her collarbone. Shivers tingled up her spine. "You said you needed to talk and you seem…heavyhearted now. I don't want to take advantage of your vulnerability, Clementine."

Cold water poured on her head. "Meaning you want me but not in the morning." She hadn't actually meant to say that, but it had been bursting inside her and had come out.

"Meaning I want you desperately and I'm just not sure of anything else," he said. "My life has been turned upside down, Clem. I told you about the con-woman. I told you about the letter. I've told you everything. My ability to trust is this big," he said, putting his thumb and forefinger very close together. "I want you. But I'm not willing to hurt you again. You want love and romance and marriage and happily-ever-after. I don't believe in any of that anymore."

She let out a sigh and pulled back a bit. At least he cared about her, she realized. He might not love her, might not want her in his life that way, but he clearly cared about her. And since they were now connected not only by the twins but by Phoebe, neither of them could walk away so easily.

She stepped back farther, putting some necessary distance between them. "Today was pretty intense," she said, changing the subject. She'd come here to talk about today anyway, not to kiss Logan. Not to be held by him. Not to hold out hope for something he'd told her time and again couldn't be.

Wouldn't be.

"Agreed," he said. "Almost too intense for me. Once I picked up the boys from school I tried not to think about anything else but them, to be present for them. But they've been asleep for a few hours now and everything's been going through my mind." He turned to the counter, adding a spoonful of sugar just the way she liked, then reaching into the refrigerator for the cream and adding a splash in each mug.

"So you're okay with being a big stepbrother?" She'd been so touched when he'd told Phoebe that their connection counted. It meant the world to Phoebe.

He handed her the yellow mug. "Not really, Clem. I'm just trying to live by the new rule of what is *is*. Truth is truth. In a roundabout way I don't like, I am her stepbrother. So I said it counted."

She stared at him, the strain in his voice making her realize just how not okay he was with it. "You seemed at peace with it when you were talking to Phoebe." But of course he wasn't. That was her wishful thinking, hoping for what might be.

He didn't respond and she knew they both could use a break from the conversation. She reached for the box of treats her grandmother had given her, setting two cookies on a napkin. She handed him one and he bit into it.

"Who made this?" he asked. "It's amazing."

She smiled. "This is from a batch that Phoebe made with Georgia, Hurley's head baker."

"Well, tell your sister I said she's an amazing pastry chef." He took a sip of his tea, then sat down at the square wooden table by the window and gestured to the seat across from his. "I'll be honest, Clementine. I'm *not* at peace with this stepbrother thing. I don't want to consider Parsons my biological father. So I don't want to consider his stepdaughter my stepsister. Does that make sense?"

She sat down and put her mug on the table. "Yeah. It does." Of course it did. She might not like it, but it made sense. She understood why he felt that way.

"But I am at peace with *one* thing," he said, "one very important thing, and I guess it helps make everything else easier to swallow."

She leaned forward, curious. "What?"

"I ran into Delia Cooper today in the grocery store. She lives next door to the ranch I grew up on. She and my mother were friendly, but I wasn't sure if she would know anything about my mother's personal life. Turns out she did. My father *did* know I wasn't his biological child."

As she listened to him talk about everything Delia had said, she could see that same sense of peace that had been on Phoebe's face on his face now as he spoke about something that tilted the world on its axis for him again.

"Oh, Logan," she said, reaching for his hand, so moved by the story of his father proposing to the woman he'd always loved, taking responsibility for another's man child and vowing to raise that child as his own. "That's a beautiful history."

"It definitely helped me feel more okay about the whole mess. I know more about my history. And there are no secrets—Phoebe knows how we're connected. Everything is more out in the open instead of hidden away. Sometimes I do want to sweep it all back under the rug, but then sometimes I really do know it's best it's not. I hate secrets."

Clementine nodded. "Me too. You did Phoebe a huge service today, Logan. You changed her life. Heck, I think you fixed her heart in a lot of ways."

He leaned back in his chair, clearly uncomfortable with the train of conversation.

"I do wish she responded to me the way she does to you," she said, sipping her tea and wrapping her hands around the comforting warmth of the mug. "I know that's small of me to be…envious. But I do wish we had that same kind of closeness."

"She'll come around, Clem. You know that, right?"

Clementine wasn't so sure. "You're just such a natural father figure. You took on the boys straight from the rodeo circuit. You'd never even been around kids before. And here you are, raising them without a hitch."

He raised an eyebrow. "The first two months I was scared to death of my nephews. And scared of failing them. I didn't know what I was doing."

"But you did everything right. Like I said, you're a natural. You just seem to get how to act and talk around kids."

"Clementine, you're running the kids' Christmas show. Of course you know what you're doing with kids."

"I have a lot of help. I thought I was good with kids from all the babysitting I do. But I can't seem to connect with Phoebe at all. She won't talk to me. She gives one-word answers and I always get the sense she wants me to leave her alone." Tears started pricking Clementine's eyes and she blinked them away.

"Hey," he said, reaching a hand over to squeeze hers. "It's just gonna take time, Clem. Maybe she's just afraid to get too close to you. One word from you and she's gone, just like with Mrs. Nivens. Just like with her aunt. Just like with her mother."

Clementine's eyes welled with tears as she wondered if that was true. It broke her heart to think that the sweet girl had internalized her fear to that degree. Clementine tried to blink back the tears, but they came slipping down her cheeks anyway. She covered her face in her hands and felt Logan wrapping his arms around her.

"It's going to be okay," he said. "Just give it time and remember you can't rush some things."

She wanted to just stay in his arms, to feel his strength, his belief in her and that everything really would work out, but Logan was going to smash her heart to smithereens and she didn't think she could bear it.

Her heart was already always on the verge of breaking because of how much she wanted to forge a strong relationship with Phoebe and how much the girl backed away from her. Trying to win Logan's love too? She couldn't even try anymore. First of all, she shouldn't have to try. Second, he'd already broken her heart once.

She had to let go of the dream of a future with Logan. He didn't want her in his life. He'd told her so tonight.

"I'd better get going," she said, rushing up. "Oh—I almost forgot to ask for the cap."

He eyed her, then stood up. They headed toward the door and he reached for the baseball cap on a peg. "If I can help," he said, "bridge the gap or make things easier, just call me." He handed her the cap.

I wish we could just be one big happy family, she thought. *You, me, the boys and Phoebe.* Clementine hadn't had a Christmas wish in so long, so many years. But now she did. A wish that wasn't going to come true.

From now on, she had to distance herself from Logan Grainger. She'd allow Phoebe all the time with him that Logan permitted, of course, but she wouldn't look for him at rehearsal drop-off and pickup anymore. She wouldn't let herself think about him, wouldn't let herself drift off to sleep fantasizing about him.

She had to let him go.

As the weeks passed, Clementine focused on building her relationship with Phoebe, teaching her how to cook the way her mother had taught Clementine, making omelets and burgers and desserts, helping her with fourth-grade projects and studying for quizzes, taking her shopping for clothes and admiring how Phoebe stuck with her own style, despite the mean-spirited teasing of Emily Catwaller, whom she'd learned to ignore. Plus, they spent three evenings a week at rehearsal together. Working on the show was a labor of love and everyone was enjoying themselves, from running through the show top to bottom to digging out the backdrops from years past and setting everything up on the stage. Clementine wasn't able to volunteer at the foster home as often as she had before, but Louisa was thrilled that Clementine had become a foster mother herself and more than once had offered sage advice to Clementine. The advice was the same from everyone: *give it time.* Somehow over the past few weeks, Clementine's mantra went from enthusiastic trumpets to broken record.

And three more times, she'd taken Phoebe over to Logan's to learn the ropes of working on a cattle ranch, each time in a different area—first was the cattle, then the barn, then the land itself. Logan had even promised Clementine he'd continue her horseback riding lessons since that was the way to start learning how to be a bronc rider. The girl idolized Logan, and she tended to make it easy for him to be around her by not talking about anything but the ranch and the rodeo.

It was interesting to Clementine that Phoebe didn't talk much about Clyde with Logan; in fact, she'd only mention him in the most casual way, such as, *Oh yeah, Clyde once told me that bull riding is all about staying grounded on the bull's back and keeping your core balance—that means focusing on your grip and your hips.* Logan always seemed charmed by how much Phoebe knew about bull riding. But she tended not to say personal things about Clyde, and while Clementine was surprised about that, Logan seemed relieved at the end of every "work" week with Phoebe.

And still, the distance between Clementine and Phoebe remained. Clementine was beginning to accept it. Three weeks wasn't that long. She might have to give up Logan Grainger ever loving her, ever wanting a future with her, but she'd never give up on Phoebe and breaking through the brick wall. Never.

Now, as Clementine waited for Phoebe in front of the elementary school so they could walk to the Blue Gulch Children's Christmas Spectacular dress rehearsal together, Phoebe said, "Do you think we could make a stop at Blue Gulch Gifts? I finally earned enough money to buy what I was saving up for."

"Sure," Clementine said. She was dying to know what it was, then realized it was probably a Christmas present for Logan.

They headed down Blue Gulch Street, passing the smoothie shop and coffee shop and the library and finally reached the gift shop. "Would you like me to come in with you or do you want some privacy?"

"I'll be fine on my own," Phoebe said.

Clementine wasn't surprised to hear that. Fifteen minutes later, Clementine almost went in to look for Phoebe and let her know they had to get to the rehearsal, but a minute later Phoebe was back with a small bag. "I'll put it in my backpack to keep it safe," she said, kneeling down on the sidewalk and carefully sliding the bag in.

"I'm glad you were able to buy what you wanted. You worked hard for that money."

Phoebe glanced up at her and smiled, but didn't say another word until they arrived at the town hall and she ran ahead with some girls she'd become friends with. It was no surprise to Clementine that Emily Catwaller had not auditioned for the Christmas show.

Tonight was a big night for the kids and everyone was excited: it was the final dress rehearsal, and then tomorrow night, the curtain would rise. The show, then Christmas Eve in three days. It was a big week.

Inside the bustling community room, Clementine put on her official director's Santa hat and was about to go onstage to call the dress rehearsal to begin when a volunteer mentioned that their lead actress would be ten minutes late. "Let's break up into groups one last time," Clementine announced. "Run through your songs until it's time to start."

"Hi, Clementine!" Harry Grainger said with a devilish smile as he ran over from the play area. He was in his rancher costume, wearing his little brown cowboy hat and his chaps.

She scooped him up and tickled his belly, then set him down. "Where, oh where could your brother be, I wonder?" She heard a familiar giggle from behind her, then leaned down and scooped up Henry, giving him a tickle too. "You boys head over to your group. Do you see Miss Sarah over there?" Clementine asked, pointing.

"I see her!" Harry said.

"I saw her first!" Henry said and they beelined over.

God, she adored those boys. She watched them for a moment, trying not to think about their handsome uncle, then was overcome with the sensation that someone was watching her. She followed the feeling until her gaze landed on her birth mother.

Over the past month, Clementine had been glad that Lacey Woolen only showed up to volunteer once a week. Whenever Lacey would enter the community room, Clementine would be aware of her to the point of distraction, despite the fact that Lacey avoided her at rehearsals. The usual, Clementine would think. Close but not too close. There, but not there in a way that would bridge the gap between them. These days, Clementine's heart, mind and soul were occupied with bridging the gap between herself and a certain nine-year-old girl whom she adored, but Lacey Woolen still managed to upend her.

She looked at Lacey sitting in the back row, full-on stared at the woman, and Lacey looked away. She was going to have to let Lacey go too, she knew. Just like she'd been trying so hard to let Logan go. He was never out of her thoughts, but she tried to push him out whenever he muscled his way in with an image of his handsome face or a memory of something kind he'd said or done.

Yes—she was going to have to let her birth mother go. And that was on Clementine, something she had to do inside herself; it had nothing to do with Lacey Woolen at all, involved no conversation, no heart-to-heart. First of all, Lacey didn't do heart-to-hearts. Second, if Clementine needed Phoebe to accept hard truths about her life, then Clementine herself needed to start doing the same. Lacey would never be accessible and that was simply that.

The determination, the decision, helped her get her mind off her birth mother and on to the rehearsal. Their young lead actress should be here any minute. Except just when the girl walked in the door with a big *sorry!*, Louisa came over and reported that one of the counselors for the eight-to-ten-year-olds had called in sick just as the other counselor staggered over looking pale and said she wasn't feeling well. Clementine sent the poor counselors home and hoped they'd feel better tomorrow, if not by Christmas. In the meantime, she had no choice but to assign herself and Lacey to work with Phoebe's group.

The thought made her kind of uneasy, but she put the three of them together, directing the small, always boisterous group of kids to the back row where Lacey sat. Phoebe's expression didn't change as she sat down two seats away from Lacey. Clementine had introduced the two the first week that Phoebe came to Blue Gulch. Watching her birth mother and her foster child assess each other during that introduction had been a very strange thing. Since then, Phoebe was quiet around Lacey and tended to move away whenever the woman came near. Clementine had expected questions from Phoebe about Lacey, about what it was like to have her birth mother living right in the same town, but Phoebe had never brought her up. Clementine wasn't entirely sure if Phoebe was avoiding asking or really wasn't interested.

"Clementine, can I go get a drink of water?" Joey Parker asked, pulling her out of her thoughts. The nine-year-old was one of Clementine's best singers. "I need to water my voice."

"Me too!" another boy said.

At Clementine's okay, the entire group of eight-to-ten-year-olds followed Joey to the water fountain on the far side of the room. Except Phoebe. She stayed where she was at the end of the row, Clementine next to her, and Lacey on the other side of Clementine.

Phoebe leaned forward and looked at Lacey. "Is it weird to know you have a daughter that someone else raised?"

Clementine gasped. Where the heck had that come from? Phoebe had barely said two words to Lacey in the past month. "Phoebe, I—"

Lacey held up a hand, pushing her long dark braid behind her shoulder. "No, her question is a fair one. And it's one of the great things about kids, isn't it? That they say what's on their minds, say it straight."

"So is it weird?" Phoebe asked, her voice flat. "I mean, don't you wish things were different even though you're the one who made them the way they are. The way they were?"

So Phoebe was interested. Of course she was. She'd been holding back, the way she'd held back with Clementine, but something in her burst free tonight.

To Phoebe, Lacey represented her own mother, Clementine realized. She wanted her questions answered. Once and for all.

Please say the right things, Lacey, whatever those things are, Clementine thought. When Clementine had asked her questions over the years, Lacey mostly avoided answering directly. Clementine had no idea what her birth mother would say. She glanced around, glad the other kids had gone to the water fountain, glad for all the singing in the room. No one could hear their conversation.

"It *is* weird," Lacey said. "It's weird and it hurts in a very deep place. But when Clementine was a kid, I couldn't take care of her. I wanted to, but sometimes, something even stronger than my love for Clementine gripped me and took over."

"My mom isn't even really my mom anymore," Phoebe said, her voice low and sad. "I know she's not coming for Christmas. She's never coming back."

Clementine blinked back her tears. She wanted to break into the conversation, but she knew she should stay silent. Right now, Phoebe and Lacey could do more for each other than Clementine could by putting in her own thoughts.

"I'm so sorry to hear that," Lacey said. "I wanted to be a mother, a good mother, to Clementine. But I couldn't. No matter how much I wanted to in my heart. You want to know something?"

"What?" Phoebe asked a little nervously.

"I loved Clementine with all my heart when she was born. When she was two and five and eight—when I terminated my parental rights so that another mother could be what I couldn't be," she whispered. "It doesn't mean I didn't love her. I did. And I do."

Clementine stared at Lacey. She'd never heard the woman say anything like that before.

"Do you think my mother loves me?" Phoebe asked Lacey.

"Yes," Lacey said, and Clementine's heart almost burst out of her chest. She had said the right thing for sure. "I'm one hundred percent sure of it."

"Well, I don't believe that," Phoebe said. "You're here. You've always been here. My mother left and that was it." Her face crumpled and she shot up and ran right through the door.

Oh no. Clementine rushed over to Louisa and asked her to take over the rehearsal, then went running out the door, Lacey behind her.

They stopped by the huge Christmas tree, looking in every direction. There was no sign of Phoebe. They ran around to the back of the town hall to the playground, but she wasn't on the tire swings or at the top of the slide or behind any of the trees or sitting along the fence.

"Let's split up," Lacey said. "Whoever finds her texts the other."

Clementine nodded, her heart beating out of her chest. "Okay. And thank you."

They rushed back around the building, Lacey heading across Blue Gulch Street, looking all around.

Clementine started up the other side of the street, glancing in the doorways, hoping to see that little face she'd come to love so much, those dear hazel eyes. But she didn't see Phoebe anywhere.

She pulled her out her cell phone and punched in Logan's number.

"Everything okay with the twins?" he asked.

"Yes. But Phoebe ran off in tears," she said in one breath. "I'm so scared, Logan. I can't find her anywhere."

"I'm on my way," he said and for a moment, relief flooded her until she spun around, looking in all directions for the child who'd become her daughter and was nowhere in sight. "We'll find her."

We'll find her, she repeated to herself. *Everything is going to be okay*, she added, trying to hold on to Logan's promise.

* * *

Logan had checked everywhere he could think for Phoebe, including his own ranch, not that the girl could have made it out here on her own. She was somewhere in town, somewhere near the town hall. He thought about last August, when Harry had gone missing in the woods through a torn fence on his property. Detective Nick Slater, who was now married to Clementine's sister, Georgia, had noticed the silver stripe of Henry's sneakers poking out under an evergreen, and Logan had almost fainted with relief. He had to think like Detective Slater, look for orange sneakers sticking out—close to where she'd gone missing.

But he'd checked every inch of the playground behind the town hall, the shops, and had twice run into Clementine and her birth mother making their own checks. None of them had found Phoebe.

He couldn't get Clementine's frantic voice on the phone out of his head. She must be out of her mind with worry. As he was looking in the alleyway beside the coffee shop, he saw Clementine running toward him down Blue Gulch Street, panic on her face. "I can't find her anywhere. I called home, and she's not there. Gram looked in every room, every closet, the backyard—she's not there. Where could she have gone?"

Logan ran a hand through his hair, racking his brain for anything, something Phoebe might have said over the past few weeks that would give a hint about where she'd go if she was upset and wanted to get away. They'd all checked the obvious places.

Logan put his hand on Clementine's shoulder. "We'll find her."

Clementine spun around slowly, straining her neck to see, but there was no sign of Phoebe.

Where the heck would Phoebe go? *Come on, think*, he told himself. It was barely three forty-five and still light out, so at least Phoebe wasn't roaming around in the dark. But according to Clementine she'd run off in hysterical tears and a girl that upset wouldn't pay attention to where she was going. Rush hour would start soon, cars whizzing by in both directions. They had to find her.

"Wait a minute," Logan said, freezing in the middle of the sidewalk in front of the library. "I have an idea where she might be."

Clementine's eyes filled with relief. "Where?"

"Follow me," he said, hoping he was right.

Across from the town hall was a feed and supply store. During Phoebe's weekly visits to the ranch, Logan had explained to Phoebe that he sometimes ground his own feed and sometimes bought from Rancher Tate's Feed and Supply in town. He'd also mentioned last week that the owner of the shop was a rodeo fan who had a big framed photo of Crazy Joe and some other famed rodeo bulls on the wall above the cattle feed bags. The shop was large and there were places a slight girl of nine could hide between huge sacks of feed and tack supplies.

"The feed store?" Clementine said as he led the way inside.

He nodded. "I just have a feeling."

The shop wasn't very busy at just before four o'clock. Holding on to Clementine's hand, he led the way to the cattle section, looking for those orange sneakers between huge sacks.

Bingo.

All that was visible were those orange sneakers and the bottoms of her jeans. She was wedged in the narrow aisle between bags of feed, sitting directly beneath Crazy Joe's photo in a gold frame.

He upped his chin at the sneakers and Clementine looked over and covered her mouth with her hand. Then she flew into his arms and whispered, "Thank you."

"Phoebe?" she called out, her voice soft. "It's me, Clementine. And Logan. We were so worried about you when you ran off."

"How'd you find me?" she asked, staying put.

"Logan had a pretty good idea that since you were upset, you might want to be with your buddy Crazy Joe and since a picture of him was the closest thing to the town hall, he thought you might come here."

Clementine looked at him as if wanting his assurance that she was on the right track. He nodded. She didn't need his help, but Clementine didn't know that yet.

He hung back as Clementine inched closer and sat down beside the bag of feed, her eyes on Phoebe's sneakers. The girl was wedged in so far against the wall that they couldn't even see her face.

"Phoebe, I'm sorry the conversation you had with Lacey upset you. Want to come out and we'll talk about it? Lacey's worried sick about you. She asked me to text her when I found you."

Phoebe inched out halfway and Logan could see her face. She looked up at him and tears welled in her eyes, then her gaze stayed on her sneakers. "I thought if I didn't talk about anything, if I didn't think about anything, that all the sad things I think about would just go away. I could just pretend they didn't exist."

"I know what you mean," Clementine said, and Logan had the sense she was holding her breath.

"But when I saw Lacey sitting right next to you, I couldn't help myself. I wanted to know stuff. I want to understand." She burst into tears and Clementine reached in for Phoebe's hand.

Logan waited, holding his own breath, hoping Phoebe would take Clementine's hand. He had a feeling she would. Time seemed to crawl.

And then there was a sob and the girl leaped out into Clementine's arms, crying, her shoulders trembling.

"It's okay to want to know," Clementine said, brushing stands of hair away from her wet cheeks. "Talking about your deepest thoughts is good for you, Phoebe. Talking about what bothers you, what scares you, what hurts you is the way to make things better."

Phoebe wiped at her eyes with her forearm. "Do you want to know why I told you I didn't want you to call me Phoebes the way my mother used to and Clyde did sometimes?"

Logan recalled Clementine telling him about the conversation, and the expression in her eyes had said all he'd needed to know about how much it had hurt Clementine.

"Why?" Clementine asked.

"Because everyone who called me Phoebes went away," Phoebe said. "That's why I'm scared to like you too much." She started crying again and looked down at the floor, the forearm going up again to wipe away tears.

Oh, Phoebe, Logan thought, his heart clenching in his chest.

Clementine's eyes welled. "I can understand that. Both things. But I promise you, Phoebe Pike, I'm not going anywhere. And you're not going anywhere. I love you. I love you very much."

"I love you too," Phoebe wailed and wrapped her arms around Clementine.

Logan let out one long breath.

Phoebe pushed her hair out of her face and looked at Clementine. "Do you remember when you asked if I might want a dog and I said no?"

Clementine nodded. "Yup, I remember. It was the day Annabel had her beagle over in the front yard.

"I didn't mean it. I've always wanted a dog. My whole life. Clyde said he would have taken me to the shelter to adopt one, but he was allergic to dogs and cats and even gerbils and hamsters."

Logan felt himself stiffen at the little anecdote about Clyde Parsons. He hadn't expected that reaction. When the hell would the man's name engender anything but acid in his gut?

Clementine smiled at Phoebe. "Well, I understand why you said no at first. And I think a trip to the county shelter is in order. It'll be wonderful to adopt a dog for Christmas."

Phoebe gave a tremulous smile. "Speaking of Christmas, would it be all right if I give you the present I bought you even though Christmas isn't for a few days?" Phoebe said. "It's your Christmas present, but I want to give it to you now."

"The present you bought this afternoon in the gift shop was for me?" Clementine asked, her eyes registering her surprise.

Phoebe nodded and reached into the narrow aisle between huge feed sacks for her backpack and pulled out a small gift bag. She handed it to Clementine.

So that was the important something she was saving up for, Logan realized. A Christmas present for her foster mother. For Clementine.

Clementine bit her lip, then pulled out a small wrapped box. She unwrapped it, put the paper in the bag and then set down the bag on one of the feed sacks. She held a small red velvet box. She opened it and gasped, her hand flying to her mouth. "Oh, Phoebe, this is beautiful."

"Turn it over," Phoebe said.

Clementine turned it over and Logan could see tears welling again.

"Well, when do I get to see what it is?" Logan asked with a smile.

Clementine laughed and held up a silver necklace with a heart-shaped pendant engraved with *Mother*. On the back was engraved, *For CH with love, PP.*

Logan glanced from the necklace to Phoebe, very aware of what this would mean to Clementine. "That's a beautiful gift, Phoebe."

Phoebe beamed.

Clementine nodded and fastened the gift around her neck, then reached a hand up to touch it. "I'll always treasure this, Phoebe. We're *family*."

"Family," Phoebe said, flinging herself back into Clementine's arms and wrapping her arms around her.

Logan stood there, realizing he was stepping backward to the point that he'd moved across the aisle. Family. The word echoed in Logan's head. Family. Family. Family.

His family had been the Graingers. His parents. His brother. His nephews. They were his family. Not some stranger who'd done one nice thing in his life. Phoebe Pike wasn't his stepsister. She was Parsons's stepdaughter.

He thought of his mother crying on the swing behind the town hall, alone and pregnant and betrayed. His maternal grandparents betrayed by the ranch hand to whom they'd offered room and board and employment. Clyde Parson had walked out on his mother without a care if she or her baby—his baby—were okay. He'd let another man step in, step up and take responsibility for what was his.

If Clyde Parsons hadn't walked away, you wouldn't have been raised by Haywood Grainger, he realized, the thought slamming into his head. *He wouldn't have been your father. He would have been an acquaintance of your mother's, a man she never knew had secretly pined for her for years.*

His entire life until four months ago would have been very, very different.

My father was Haywood Grainger, he told himself. *That's all I need to know.*

He needed to get out of here. He needed to breathe.

"I'd better get back to the ranch," he said. "I'll come by rehearsal to pick up the boys."

"Okay," Clementine said, tilting her head at him. *She knows,* he realized, *that I can't do this. Can't pretend that Phoebe and I are a family, can't deal with it.* Because it would mean accepting what he still refused to accept, no matter what the hell he said about the truth.

Clementine had kept herself scarce the past few weeks, barely speaking to him during the two hours Phoebe had spent at the ranch each week, smiling politely when he'd pick up or drop off the twins, which he'd found himself doing because she was acting so… distant. Now he just wanted to escape from her again.

He wanted to go home to his nephews and the world he'd created for them, a Grainger world where Clyde Parsons didn't exist.

But Phoebe made him exist just by being. And she and Clementine were now a package deal.

But besides, Clementine wanted more from him than he could ever give. His ability to believe in love and trust and happy endings had been obliterated.

"See you at pickup," he repeated, hating how he was ruining a beautiful moment between Clementine and Phoebe by being so shut down.

He managed a smile to Phoebe, who smiled back, and again the urge to get away was stronger than anything else he felt.

Chapter Ten

Part of her Christmas wish had come true, Clementine realized as she pulled up to Logan's house later that night. She and Phoebe *were* a family. And Clementine had made good on her hope to surprise her grandmother with an outdoor dining room in the garden. Essie's Christmas gift wouldn't be finished until early spring, but the carefully drawn plans and contract were rolled up with a big red bow, and Clementine knew her grandmother would love it.

Two Christmas wishes down. One to go.

Logan wasn't expecting her. He'd picked up the twins at the end of rehearsal, but because it had been the final one, she was bombarded by kids and counselors and volunteers with questions and lost costume pieces and little fires to put out. She hadn't had a chance to even talk to Logan. Out of the corner of her eye she'd seen him wave to Phoebe, who'd been sitting with her friends, singing their showstopper hymn one last time before the Spectacular tomorrow night. Then he'd left and she'd felt so strangely bereft—as if she'd ever really had him at all.

She reached a hand up to touch the necklace Phoebe had given her. *Mother* engraved on the front of the heart, their initials on the back. Clementine's own heart had opened wide because of the gift. She was being entrusted with a child's heart. And she was going to take very good care of it.

But Logan had made it clear in that feed shop that he didn't want to be entrusted with either of their hearts. That he was never planning on being part of that family—either as Phoebe's big brother or as Clementine's husband.

She needed to let him go once and for all. Let the dream of him go. She'd tried the past few weeks by simply avoiding him, but avoiding wasn't the same as "handling" or "dealing with." She had to ask him the question burning in her gut and if the answer was *can't, sorry*, she would walk away.

She needed him to say it to her face tonight so that she knew, for absolutely sure, that when asked directly, when asked to make a choice between having her in his life or not, his answer was *not*. She expected no different. Then she'd try to move on. She was done trying to read into things, read minds. She wanted to hear it from the man himself.

She walked up to the porch, glancing over at the cattle in the pastures, at Crazy Joe standing in the dark, another bull by his side. She smiled at him and telepathically told him that Phoebe sent her love, that Clementine owed him one, and then she gently knocked on the door, knowing that the twins were asleep.

Logan opened the door, surprise in his blue eyes. He had to look so damned handsome, didn't he? He wore a long-sleeved green henley shirt and jeans and he filled the doorway with all six feet two inches of him. "I wasn't expecting you."

"I know and I'm sorry for just coming over. But I need to know something for sure. I don't want to come in. I just want to know, to hear it from your lips right now."

"Hear what?" he asked, but she was sure he knew exactly what she was talking about. He shoved his hands in the pockets of his jeans, his expression wary. And weary.

Just say it, Clem. Say it and you'll know, one way or the other.

She couldn't help glancing up at the night sky, catching a star and making a wish. But she wouldn't hold out too much hope. Not after how he'd reacted in the feed store.

She cleared her throat. "I need to know if I should give up on you, Logan Grainger. Give up on the dream of us. A future."

Logan stepped back and something crossed his features that she couldn't read. It was a look that said *don't push me.* But push him, she had to. "I care about you, Clementine. You know that."

"I care about you, Clementine, *but,*" she said. "I need to hear the but so I can walk away. Because I can't do this anymore, Logan. It's tearing me apart. And I need to focus on Phoebe. I can't have a worried heart all the time. Either you love me or you don't."

He crossed his arms over his chest again. "It's not that simple."

"Yes, it is."

He ran a hand through his hair. "Can't you come in and we can talk?"

She wasn't leaving this porch. "Do we have a future, Logan?"

He stared at her, then those broad shoulders sagged. "I—I—" He ran a hand through his hair, clearly unwilling to finish what he'd been about to say.

She lifted her chin. "Goodbye, then. I'll be cordial when I see you. I know that Phoebe will want to keep working for you, so at this point, given that she's been here for a month, I feel comfortable dropping her off so that I don't need to stick around. And now that Phoebe and I have had our breakthrough, you can think of her as my foster daughter and not as your stepsister. That should help."

He just stared at her and didn't say a word.

"Goodbye, Logan," she said, her heart breaking. "You are being a *wouldn't*. Because I've seen you in *could* action. You're choosing to be alone, choosing to hold on to the bitter part of a truth that you could accept if you'd allow yourself to, if you'd just live by what you preached to Phoebe weeks ago in that pony pasture."

"Can't," Logan said. "Not won't."

She shook her head. "You're choosing bitterness over love, Logan Grainger. And semantics aside, that's just plain wrong."

She blinked back the tears in her eyes, turned around and walked away, but her heart came with her this time. Broken, but not left behind.

* * *

Clementine waited at Blue Gulch Coffee for Lacey, not sure if the woman would really show up. After Logan had left the feed store yesterday, Clementine had finally texted Lacey that she'd found Phoebe and all was well. There was so much more she'd wanted to say to Lacey, so much she wanted to talk about after all Lacey had said to Phoebe before she'd run off, but she couldn't exactly text all that. And Lacey never answered her phone or her door. Clementine was done chasing people who didn't want her in their lives.

But then Lacey had shocked her by showing up at Hurley's this morning while Clementine was working on the Creole sauce for the Christmas buffet. She asked if they could meet for coffee later that afternoon and talk. Clementine had almost fainted with shock.

But Lacey was ten minutes late. Then fifteen minutes late. Then twenty minutes late. Clementine got up, ready to give up. Lacey had done a world of good for Clementine yesterday; she'd provided the catalyst to break apart the barriers between her and Phoebe. But all those things she'd said about how she felt about Clementine, how she'd always felt, how she felt now, had deeply touched Clementine. Lacey was who she was, who she'd always been. It was time to accept it.

As Clementine was about to leave, she saw Lacey coming up Blue Gulch Street in her long skirt and cowboy boots and the tan suede jacket. Lacey stopped and turned around, and Clementine was pretty sure she was going to keep going in the other direction, but then she turned around again and came inside.

Clementine sat down and smiled at Lacey, and Lacey gave a tight smile back and came over to the table.

"I'm glad you're here," Clementine said. "I know it's not easy for you."

Lacey sat down. "I would love a cup of coffee. I hear the pumpkin spice is really good."

Clementine nodded. "It is. The peppermint mocha too."

If Lacey could only talk coffee flavors, then Clementine would talk coffee flavors. That was fine. It was finally fine.

They walked to the counter and both ordered the pumpkin spice. When the barista handed Lacey her cup, Lacey took a sip and said it was as good as she'd heard.

"I can't stay," Lacey added. "I'm…sorry."

"That's all right," Clementine said. And it was. "I hope I'll see you tonight at the children's Christmas show. You were such a big help."

"I'll be there," Lacey said.

She had no doubt Lacey would come and sit on the aisle in the row of chairs closest to the door. Sometimes, you really did have to let people be who they were, take them on their terms. Sometimes, those terms were unacceptable, like Logan's. It all depended. Clementine understood that now.

"And I hope you'll come to the Christmas buffet at Hurley's on Christmas Eve," Clementine said as she walked Lacey to the door. "Phoebe and I will save a spot for you at our table. But I'll understand if you can't come."

Lacey smiled and hurried away. For the first time ever, Clementine watched her birth mother walk away without feeling bereft or wanting something out of reach.

* * *

At high noon, Logan sat in the stands at the Stock-town Rodeo, watching an old rival—not *the* rival, though—trying his best to stay on Desperado, a gor-geous black bull who had tossed the past three riders on their butts. Logan wore sunglasses and his Stetson, not wanting to be recognized, whether as Logan Grainger, three-time champ or worse, as the Handcuff Cowboy.

He wasn't even sure why he'd come. He'd woken up this morning with Clementine's face, the pain in her eyes, the things she'd said…*you've chosen bitterness over love*…and he'd called Karen to take care of the boys today since they were out of school for the next two weeks and then he'd driven out to Stocktown.

He'd passed through Tuckerville, purposely driving past the steak house where he'd taken the con-woman a bunch of times. Driving past the hotel where he'd been betrayed like a chump instead of a champ. Driv-ing past the hospice and then the foster home where he and Clementine had met Phoebe for the first time. Mrs. Nivens had been on the porch again, a bunch of kids sit-ting around her as they decorated Christmas stockings.

Then he'd driven to Stocktown and bought a ticket to the rodeo, sitting through all the events, from bronc riding to steer roping to bull riding. The rodeo clown had made him laugh and fear for the guy's life; the job took guts and skill and had his full respect, despite what Phoebe's former foster mother had thought.

"That's my boy coming out next," the man one seat over from Logan said, nodding in greeting. "Bull rider. He's never lasted eight seconds, but he keeps trying. Gotta hand it to him."

Logan nodded back, glancing at the middle-aged man wearing a tan Stetson. "Not easy. I used to ride. Nice of you to come out and support your son. Some parents get nervous about seeing their children, full-grown adults, on bulls and stay away."

The man's brows furrowed. "Well, I do worry about him, but I don't get to see him otherwise. We've got our problems. Never seen eye to eye. But up here, I can just be his father, you know? No talking, no fighting, no arguing."

Up here I can just be his father.

Logan turned to face the man, something inside him shifting. He imagined Clyde Parsons up here event after event, watching his biological son on the back of a bucking bull, thinking for those eight seconds, I *am* Logan's father.

He suddenly understood why Clyde had come to his events. Why he'd spoken so proudly about him to Phoebe. Why he'd saved the scrapbook of Logan's accomplishments. He understood why he'd written the letter.

Clyde Parsons had done wrong and had tried in the ways he could to make it right by putting those one and five dollar bills in the PO box week after week for eighteen years. Then, when he knew he was dying, he had to make amends with his own heart, mind and soul, *and* the child he'd walked away from. So he'd said his *I'm sorry* in the letter, a goodbye in lieu of ever having said hello.

It hadn't been a grenade dropped in a life or a terrible parting gift. It had been a true *I'm sorry that I couldn't and wouldn't.*

"Call your son after his event," Logan said to the

man. "Tell him you're here. Tell him you're proud of him, that you love him. You don't have to say anything else." He stood up and headed toward the aisle.

"Maybe I'll do just that," the man said.

"No maybe," Logan said. "Just do it. Could change two lives today and your entire future."

He left the stands and headed for his car. He had a Children's Christmas Spectacular to get his boys to. Then a woman to see. To try to right some wrongs of his own.

The town hall community room was standing room only for the Blue Gulch Children's Christmas Spectacular. When Logan and the twins arrived, their counselor waved Harry and Henry over and hurried them backstage. He looked around for an empty seat, hoping to avoid the back rows so he could have a decent view.

"Logan! Up here."

He glanced in the direction of Phoebe's voice. She was waving from the front row, all dressed up in her shepherd girl costume. He walked over to her and she pointed to a sign she'd made with his name on the center seat. A nicely drawn lasso was on either side of his name.

"I saved you the best seat," she said.

He smiled at her. "I owe you one. Thanks."

As he looked at Phoebe, he saw a sweet nine-year-old girl who happened to be the stepdaughter of his biological father. Which made her his kid stepsister. Now, it felt like more than just a truth, a fact. It just *was*. And it was finally okay with him.

"Wait till you see how adorable Harry and Henry are in the show," she said. "They're singing in two different ensembles and they're onstage often as back-ground ranchers."

He couldn't wait to see them in their first Christmas show. "I know they've loved the rehearsals. Thanks for being such a good friend to them."

She smiled. "Well, I'd better get backstage. See ya."

The lights blinked to indicate that everyone should take their seats, then Clementine came onstage, looking so beautiful in a red dress, her long brown hair loose around her shoulders. She thanked everyone for com-ing and talked a bit about how hard the kids had worked and how wonderful it was to work with them. Then the lights dimmed even more and Clementine hurried down the stage steps…right to the empty seat beside him. Well, it was empty except for a stack of folders.

"Oh!" she said, clearly surprised. She picked up the folders and that's when he saw a sign with her name on it. Hearts were on either side of her name.

"Phoebe saved the seat for me," he said, drinking in the sight of her. "I didn't realize she put me right next to you." *I owe you, again, Phoebe.*

"Ah." She sat down and they were so close he could smell her shampoo. Their knees bumped once, and she shifted over.

"I could move to the back if you prefer," he said, un-able to drag his gaze away from her profile.

She glanced at him, clearly uncomfortable having him so close. "No, of course not. It's fine."

The curtain rose and he could tell she was relieved not to have to make awkward small talk with him.

For the next forty-five minutes, the Christmas Spectacular was equal parts moving, funny, serious and beautiful. The youngest groups sang "Jingle Bells" without a hitch.

When the curtain closed, there was a standing ovation and the kids came out onstage for a bow, Clementine joining them. Many parents and kids gave her roses and bouquets of flowers, including Harry and Henry, who'd taken the wildflowers they'd picked from their property backstage with them when they'd arrived.

Finally, the room began clearing out. Phoebe was chatting animatedly to a bunch of girls who'd been with her in the show, and the twins were playing a board game in the children's play area, so Logan took the opportunity to speak to Clementine alone. She was straightening chairs in the back row and picking up the few "Playbills" some people had left behind.

"Hey," he said, setting a chair back into position.

She whirled around, the flouncy hem of her red dress swishing at her knees. "You don't have to do that. I've got it."

"My pleasure after all you've done for Harry and Henry with this show. Remember a month ago when they couldn't get past the first two words of 'Jingle Bells'?"

She smiled. "They sure did come a long way."

He nodded. "I thought I'd take the boys out to Hurley's for a celebratory dinner. I was wondering if you and my stepsister would like to join us."

She froze, staring at him. "Logan Grainger? Did you just refer to Phoebe as your stepsister?"

"I went to the Stocktown rodeo today and had a few realizations as I sat in the stands. One is that Phoebe *is* my stepsister. She just is. Clyde Parson was my biological father. She was his stepdaughter. That makes her my stepsister. But you know what? Regardless of how we're connected, I happen to thinks she's an awesome kid."

"I happen to think so too," Clementine said, her beautiful brown eyes misty.

He reached up a hand to her face, unable to take his eyes off her. "So we're on for dinner?" he asked. Her heart necklace lay just above her barest hint of cleavage. She was stunning, whether in her Hurley's waitress apron or this red dress.

"We are on," she whispered, pressing her cheek against his hand.

As dinner with the Grainger men and Phoebe wound down, Clementine chatted with the boys over the crumbs of their chicken fingers and fries about their favorite parts of the Christmas show. Logan was deep in conversation with Phoebe about the kind of dog she hoped to adopt from the animal shelter tomorrow. She wanted a cute mutt, any color, maybe on the small side. She'd know the right one when she saw it. Clementine absolutely agreed.

"So Clyde was allergic to animals, huh?" she heard Logan say to Phoebe.

Clementine's head popped up from the placemat she was holding down so that Harry and Henry could draw on it with crayons. She stared at Logan, this man she loved so much, and knew his heart truly had opened.

"Yeah, but there was a dog shelter just a few blocks away from our house, and Clyde arranged for me to volunteer there in the puppy room even though just walking into the shelter made him sneeze. He'd wait in the front area while I played with the puppies. Sometimes the staff even let me name them."

"Clyde sounds like he was a good person," Logan said.

Phoebe nodded. "He was. I wish you could have known him. He told me that he'd made a lot of mistakes when he was younger that he regretted and that I should always do the right thing, even if it was hard."

Clementine watched Logan, saw him take that in.

"Well that's really good advice, a good way to live," Logan said, his blue eyes untroubled.

Phoebe smiled. "You know, it doesn't feel as bad to talk about him the way it used to."

Logan slung his arm around Phoebe. "I know just what you mean."

Clementine feared she was about to burst into happy tears so she excused herself to bring out a surprise. She went into the kitchen and loaded up a dessert cart for her table to choose from, a perk of being a Hurley and head waitress, not that she was working tonight.

"I'll babysit tonight for you," her gram said as she stirred a big pot of potato leek soup at the stove by the window.

"Babysit?" Clementine repeated, wheeling the cart over to Essie.

"Every time I peeked through the window on the door to the dining room, I saw you and Logan Grainger looking at each other like a couple madly in love."

Clementine blushed. "Well, I'm madly in love. I don't know where he stands. He's come around as far as Phoebe is concerned, with their family connection, but I'm not sure he believes in love and happy-ever-after anymore."

"Oh really?" Gram said, bringing Clementine over to the window on the door. "That's love right there."

Clementine smiled as she watched both Grainger twins sitting on their uncle's lap as he pointed out the different desserts available on the menu. Phoebe had scooted close and whatever she'd said had made him laugh.

"Love is love," Gram said. "Logan just didn't know that before."

Hope dared bloom in Clementine's heart. Her grandmother was never wrong.

At nine o'clock, Clementine sat on the big leather couch in Logan's living room, waiting for him to come downstairs from putting his nephews to bed. Earlier at Hurley's, as they'd had coffee on the porch while the kids played in the front yard, Logan said he'd like to talk to her in private, and she'd told him her grandmother had offered to babysit Phoebe, so he'd invited her over. Now, here she was, everything in her on red alert as she waited for him. Would he tell her he was still unable to give her what she wanted: a future with him?

Finally he came downstairs and sat down beside her. "The scamps are asleep. The play and dinner tuckered them out."

She smiled. And waited.

He turned to face her, taking her hands in his. "Clementine, last night you asked if you should give up on me, if we had a future. I couldn't even answer you. But now I can. Can and will."

She held her breath, waiting.

He took her hand. "I've loved you from the moment I met you, Clementine Hurley. But I was scared spitless of how much I felt for you. I'm not anymore. I love you. And I want you to be my wife."

She gasped. "Oh Logan. I loved you from the moment I met you. And I want to be your wife."

"So I guess that means you'll marry me," he said. He pulled a little velvet box from his pocket and handed it to her.

She squeezed her eyes shut for a moment, then opened them, sure this had to be a dream. But Logan was still sitting beside her, love shining in his eyes. And there was a ring box in her hands. She opened it, and a beautiful antique diamond twinkled at her.

"Will you marry me, Clementine?" he asked.

"Yes," she whispered. "I will."

He slid the ring on her finger. "In the coming days, I'd like to talk about us formally petitioning to adopt Phoebe. I know there are some complications, and of course, we'll need to talk to her first about it. But I want us to be a family. You, me, the boys and Phoebe. Officially."

Tears came to Clementine's eyes. "I think Phoebe would love that. And so would I."

He kissed her, then picked her up in his arms and carried her up the stairs. "You told me more than once that sex meant love. Well, my love, I can't wait another second."

She smiled and tilted her face up to kiss him. Neither could she.

Epilogue

Christmas Eve dinner at Hurley's Homestyle Kitchen had also turned into an engagement party for Clementine and Logan. The Hurleys and the kitchen crew were taking turns working tonight, Clementine and Dylan, the eighteen-year-old line cook and single father of sweet baby Timmy, were on the first shift with Gram. Georgia and Annabel were on second shift, and so the first shift bunch were now sitting down with their plates.

West Montgomery and Nick Slater were both helping serve on the buffet line, Clementine's handsome brothers-in-law both wearing Santa hats. Logan and Phoebe had waited for Clementine's shift to be over before heading over to the buffet, but the twins had already gobbled up their fill and were now in the children's play area, coloring.

Clementine glanced at the beautiful Christmas tree in the corner of the dining room by the big window. She smiled as she thought of the tree in Logan's living room; he'd invited Clementine and Phoebe to come help trim it today, and Clementine had brought over some extra ornaments. But when Phoebe took a small box from her backpack and pulled out two red-and-gold ornaments with her name on one and Clyde's on the other, Clementine wondered how Logan would react.

"Could I hang these on your tree?" Phoebe asked. "I think Clyde sure would like that."

"I think he would too," Logan said. "And so would I."

Phoebe looked like she might burst with happiness. She'd carefully hung the two ornaments side by side, high up enough that two active little three-year-olds couldn't reach them, and then stood back and admired them. Then she'd turned and wrapped her arms around Logan and he'd hugged her back.

"Merry Christmas," he'd said to her.

"Merry Christmas," she'd said back.

Afterward, Logan had mentioned to Clementine that he'd like to put the money Clyde had left Logan in an account for Phoebe, to be turned over to her on her eighteenth birthday. Clementine had agreed it was a lovely idea.

Clementine glanced at the two of them now; Logan was next to Clementine and Phoebe next to him, and he was explaining the history of gumbo, which he loved, and what all was in it. Phoebe wasn't sure she wanted to try it, but finally agreed to take a spoonful, then rushed over to the buffet to get her own bowl, which earned her a laugh and a *told you* from Logan.

The seat on the other side of Clementine was open; Clementine had texted Lacey that seven would be a good time to arrive, but the seat remained empty an hour later.

For the next ten minutes there was excited chatter about the new venture Hurley's Homestyle Kitchen was getting involved with: a food truck. Essie had noticed a couple of different food trucks in town—one Mexican and one featuring soup, and thought Hurley's could have its own brightly-colored food truck, offering several different kinds of po'boys. The truck would be parked at the far end of Main Street as an option for the lunch and early dinner crowd.

"Do you think Olivia Mack will say yes to running the food truck?" Logan asked Clementine.

"I hope so," Clementine said. Olivia, a lovely young woman who lived in town, had her own catering business and often helped out in the Hurley's kitchen when they were busy.

Phoebe ate a spoonful of gumbo. "Olivia is the fortune teller's daughter, right? I've heard some kids talk about Madam Miranda."

"That's right," Clementine said. So many times Clementine had thought about sneaking over to Madam Miranda's fortune-telling parlor for a reading. But she'd resisted, not sure she wanted to know anything about her future in advance.

In any case, Clementine sure hoped that Olivia would agree to operate Hurley's Homestyle Kitchen's new food truck. There was something so . . . magical about Olivia's cooking. You ate one of her po'boys or cannolis and sighed with contentment. She was *that* good.

"I hear congratulations are in order," someone said from behind her.

Clementine turned around and there was Lacey Woolen in a pretty green dress. "I'm so glad you're here, Lacey. And yes, Logan and I will be getting married on New Year's Eve! It'll just be a small ceremony for family and close friends. I hope you'll come." She saw Lacey take that in, saw that she was touched.

"I'm very happy for you both," Lacey said, noncommittal as always, but that was perfectly okay. She glanced down at the open seat beside Clementine. "Is this the seat you said you saved for me?"

Clementine nodded. She didn't expect Lacey to stay. But she was very glad she'd come, even if just to say Merry Christmas and congratulations.

And Lacey did walk away, but not toward the door. Instead, she headed over to the buffet and picked up a plate that Phoebe, now on plate-handing-out duty, gave her. Then she chose a bit of everything and came back and sat next to Clementine.

"This Creole sauce is amazing," Lacey said as she ate a spoonful of gumbo with the sauce Clementine had worked so hard to perfect. "Compliments to the chef."

Suddenly Clementine's heart was so full she wasn't sure she'd have any room for food. She looked around the table—at her birth mother, at her foster daughter, at the man who would soon be her husband, then glanced around the room and spotted her grandmother serving

at the buffet, and her sisters coming through the swing-
ing door of the kitchen with two full serving dishes of
roast turkey and garlic mashed potatoes.

As Logan reached for her hand and kissed her knuck-
les for absolutely no reason at all, earning a sweet giggle from Phoebe next to him, Clementine realized that
every one of her Christmas wishes had come true.

On New Year's Eve, Clementine, escorted by her
grandmother, walked down the aisle to her handsome
groom. Essie and Clementine's sisters had cleared out
the big dining room of Hurley's Homestyle Kitchen,
Clementine's favorite place on earth, and had trans-
formed it into a beautiful wedding venue. A narrow
silver carpet created an aisle, and there were white
flowers everywhere. The tables had been pushed to
the side and beautifully decorated, and there was a big
area meant to be a dance floor.

Clementine wore her grandmother's fifty-year-old
wedding dress, the very one her sister Annabel had
worn to marry West Montgomery in Las Vegas last
April. Georgia would have worn the dress to marry her
beloved, Detective Nick Slater, but there was no way
the dress would have fit over Georgia's very pregnant
belly. Gram hoped to pass the dress on to whomever
their wonderful cook Dylan might fall in love with
someday, and then Phoebe and then Lucy when they
grew up. Clementine adored the idea of the antique
wedding dress passing through so many different lives
and loves.

Right before she'd walked down the aisle, she'd

asked her daughter to help her put her most treasured gift around her neck. As Clementine had stood before the full-length mirror, Phoebe had tears in her eyes as she fastened the heart pendant. Clementine no longer used the word *foster* when thinking of Phoebe. There would be a bit of a road ahead of them in terms of adopting Phoebe, but the girl was her daughter in the way it counted most: in her heart.

Now, Clementine stood at the altar, about to marry the man she loved. The bridal party, Annabel, Georgia and Phoebe, looked beautiful in their deep red velvet dresses. The groomsmen, West, Nick and Dylan, looked very handsome in their tuxedos. Lucy, Annabel's stepdaughter, was the flower girl, and two little ring bearers named Harry and Henry took their duties very seriously.

In the front row sat Lacey Woolen wearing a blue dress. Essie Hurley was right next to her, and tears came to Clementine's eyes at the beautiful sight.

"How did I get so lucky?" she whispered to her groom.

"I'm the lucky one," Logan said. "You changed my life."

"I think the whole bunch of us changed our lives," Clementine said. "The twins changed yours, Phoebe changed mine, then yours, then ours."

"Yours, mine and ours. We're now just one big happy family," Logan said.

"One big happy family," Clementine repeated.

The reverend at the podium welcomed the guests and talked about love and commitment and family and the symbolism of embarking on a new year as a married couple. And finally, he asked Logan the words Clementine had longed to hear.

"Do you, Logan Grainger, take this woman to be your lawfully wedded wife, to love, honor and cherish as long as you both shall live?"

Logan took her hands in his and looked into her eyes, his blue eyes both intense and soft on her at the same time. "I do. With all my heart, I do."

Clementine ordered herself not to cry. The reverend repeated the same question to her.

"I do," she said, looking at her handsome groom. "With all my heart, I do."

"Then by the power vested in me by the state of Texas, I now pronounce you husband and wife. Feel free to kiss your bride, Logan."

Logan stepped closer and took her face in his hands, kissing her so intensely and passionately and sweetly that her knees almost buckled.

Then he stepped back just a bit and faced their guests, their loved ones, and said, "I now pronounce us family."

"Yay! We're all a family!" Harry exclaimed, rushing up to Logan and Clementine. His twin followed and both boys threw their arms around them.

With happy tears in her own eyes, Phoebe ran over to them, squeezing Clementine in a hug, then Logan, then each twin.

The guests rose to their feet, clapping and cheering, and Essie Hurley let out a wolf whistle that had everyone laughing.

Holding hands in a line, the five of them, Clementine, Logan, Phoebe, Harry and Henry walked back up the aisle together, one big happy family.

* * * * *

What happens when a fortune teller's daughter and pragmatic PI team up to find a missing person?

Find out in THE COOK'S SECRET INGREDIENT,
the next book in the delicious
HURLEY'S HOMESTYLE KITCHEN *series,*
coming in February 2017!

MILLS & BOON®

Cherish™

EXPERIENCE THE ULTIMATE RUSH OF FALLING IN LOVE

MILLS & BOON®

EXCLUSIVE EXTRACT

Crown Prince Armando enlists Rosa Lamberti to find him a suitable wife—but could a stolen kiss under the mistletoe lead to an unexpected Christmas wedding?

Read on for a sneak preview of
WINTER WEDDING FOR THE PRINCE
by Barbara Wallace

"Have you ever looked at an unfocused telescope only to turn the knob and make everything sharp and clear?" Armando asked.

Rosa nodded.

"That is what it was like for me, a few minutes ago. One moment I had all these sensations I couldn't explain swirling inside me, then the next everything made sense. They were my soul coming back to life."

"I don't know what to think," she said.

"Then don't think," he replied. "Just go with your heart."

He made it sound easy. Just go with your heart. But what if your heart was frightened and confused? For all his talk of coming to life, he was essentially in the same place as before, unable or unwilling to give her a true emotional commitment.

On the other hand, her feelings wanted to override her common sense, so maybe they were even. As she watched him close the gap between them, she felt her heartbeat quicken to match her breath.

"You do know that we're under the mistletoe yet again, don't you?"

The sprig of berries had quite a knack for timing, didn't it? Anticipation ran down her spine ceasing what little hold common sense still had. Armando was going kiss her and she was going to let him. She wanted to lose herself in his arms. Believe for a moment that his heart felt more than simple desire.

This time, when he wrapped his arm around her waist, she slid against him willingly, aligning her hips against his with a smile.

"Appears to be our fate," she whispered. "Mistletoe, that is."

"You'll get no complaints from me." She could hear her heart beating in her ears as his head dipped toward hers. "Merry Christmas, Rosa."

"Mer..." His kiss swallowed the rest of her wish. Rosa didn't care if she spoke another word again. She'd waited her whole life to be kissed like this. Fully and deeply, with a need she felt all the way down to her toes.

They were both breathless when the moment ended. With their foreheads resting against each other, she felt Armando smile against her lips. "Merry Christmas," he whispered again.

Don't miss
WINTER WEDDING FOR THE PRINCE
by Barbara Wallace

Available December 2016

www.millsandboon.co.uk

Give a 12 month subscription to a friend today!

Call Customer Services
0844 844 1358*
or visit
millsandboon.co.uk/subscriptions